Also by Michelle Schusterman

Also by Michelle Schusterman

OLIVE
and the
Backstage
GHOST

Michelle Schusterman

Random House New York

Text copyright © 2017 by Michelle Schusterman
Jacket art copyright © 2017 by Jennifer Bricking

All rights reserved. Published in the United States by Random House Children's Books, a division of Penguin Random House LLC, New York.

Random House and the colophon are registered trademarks of Penguin Random House LLC.

Visit us on the Web! randomhousekids.com

Educators and librarians, for a variety of teaching tools, visit us at RHTeachersLibrarians.com

Library of Congress Cataloging-in-Publication Data
Names: Schusterman, Michelle, author.
Title: Olive and the backstage ghost / by Michelle Schusterman.
Description: First edition. | New York : Random House, [2017] | Summary: "Olive discovers an old theater where she'll finally have a chance to shine onstage, but this theater—and its mysterious owner—are hiding dark secrets" —Provided by publisher.
Identifiers: LCCN 2015038765 | ISBN 978-0-399-55066-9 (hardcover) | ISBN 978-0-399-55067-6 (hardcover library binding) | ISBN 978-0-399-55068-3 (ebook)
Subjects: | CYAC: Theaters—Fiction. | Haunted places—Fiction. | Ghosts—Fiction.
Classification: LCC PZ7.S39834 Ol 2017 | DDC [Fic]—dc23

Printed in the United States of America
10 9 8 7 6 5 4 3 2 1
First Edition

For Edgar, you poor, troubled soul

CONTENTS

Sit in a theatre, to see
A play of hopes and fears . . .

From "The Conqueror Worm,"
by Edgar Allan Poe

OLIVE and the Backstage GHOST

1

Its Stubborn Heart

Olive Preiss thought of her city as a massive beast, and the theater district was its heart. Not a pretty heart you might doodle in a notebook, all curvy and neatly joined up at a point. More like the heart of a kraken—a raw mess of arteries and ventricles and veins clustered in the center, pumping tons of frenetic black energy through the monster.

So Olive didn't draw neat, pretty hearts. She preferred them big and messy. Kraken hearts. One side might be bigger than the other, or the ends might cross with a violent slash. Sometimes her hearts looked like a hastily scrawled letter *B,* or a lopsided 3 with a tail. Olive used to attempt to be neat, but occasionally she practiced deliberate carelessness. Yet another imperfection for her mother to pick at.

She was doodling hearts on her music folder in the car one morning as her mother drove them to the city's arts center. These hearts were more wibbly-wobbly than usual, thanks to Olive's trembling hand. When the car made a sharp turn, the resulting heart looked more like a sloppy treble clef. Olive tucked her pencil back in the folder with a sigh.

Casting a furtive glance at Mrs. Preiss, she rolled her window down a tiny bit and inhaled deeply. Olive liked how the city smelled, because it smelled like everything good and bad—fried foods, cheap cologne, trash left out a day too long. Her mother said it stank, but Olive found it complex: a full range of disgusting to delicious.

"Olive."

"Yes?"

"Where is your barrette?"

Olive's hands flew up to her windblown hair, combing through short, dark tangles for the metal barrette. She plucked it out, wincing when a few strands ripped free. The car slowed to a stop at a light, and Mrs. Preiss turned to her daughter with a disapproving frown.

"Here." She took the barrette and slid it into place, the metal scraping Olive's scalp. "And close your window. The heat causes frizzies."

Olive took her time, turning the window crank as slowly as possible.

"Do you have the forms?"

"Yes." Olive patted her music folder, wondering why Mrs. Preiss had bothered to ask. She had, after all, tucked the arts center's theater camp enrollment forms into Olive's folder herself before they left.

"And the check?"

"Yes." The slip of paper worth more than a month of bills was secured to Olive's forms with a paper clip. Non-refundable.

Mrs. Preiss cast a sharp glance at her. "How are you feeling?"

Anyone but Olive might miss the underlying threat in the question. She clasped her hands tightly. "Fine."

"This audition is important, Olive," Mrs. Preiss said, as if Olive weren't acutely aware of this fact. "Theater camp isn't worth the expense if you're just going to be an understudy, like last summer. Talent scouts won't be interested in anyone outside of the leading roles."

Olive swallowed hard and said nothing. She had enjoyed being the understudy, truth be told. There had been no reason to worry about talent scouts. And most rehearsals weren't darkened by her mother's presence, so Olive had been free to lose herself in the performance in peace. But that was last year.

A lot could change in a year.

Her mother pressed on the gas pedal, tucking a straight brown lock behind her ear. No summer humidity would dare cause Laurel Preiss's hair to frizz. "It's time to conquer this ridiculous . . . stage fright."

Stage fright. She said it with a sneer, the same contemptuous tone she reserved for words like *beggars* and *thrift stores.* Olive traced a messy heart on the window with her finger. She did not have stage fright.

"I know" was all she said.

"You love singing, Olive."

This was very true.

"You *want* to perform."

Also true.

"Most children don't have the opportunities you have. Especially these days." Mrs. Preiss squeezed the steering wheel, her knuckles whitening. "You can't let fear of the spotlight stop you."

I'm not afraid of the spotlight. Olive bit her lip and stared through the glass at a bus stop, where colorful new advertisements for the latest musicals and plays covered the outside of the shelter. The city may have been struggling to survive in the last few years, weakened by hard times, constantly on the verge of collapse. But its stubborn heart beat on.

Squinting, Olive scanned the names of the theaters. She'd heard of only a few, but that wasn't unusual. It was next to impossible to know *all* the venues in the city, and not just because of sheer number. The theaters were in constant flux, moving and changing, opening and closing. It was a feverish, never-ending search for the next big show, the next big star.

Olive dreamed about being that star. If it hadn't been for her mother, she might even have dared to believe it was possible.

2

Mother Fright

When Olive was eight, she'd spent months practicing for her first music recital. She still grew warm at the memory of the stage lights overhead, sweat blurring her vision as she listened, detached, while her own voice turned to an unrecognizable warble. The whir and flash of her father's camera in the otherwise silent crowd. Her mother's fierce gaze, more scalding than the lights.

Just a little case of stage fright, her teacher had said reassuringly. *Normal for your first recital. It'll get easier.* And that might have been true if Olive weren't the daughter of one of the city's most beloved stars.

Mrs. Preiss had been discovered by a talent scout at age ten and enjoyed a few wildly successful decades on the city's most prestigious stages. Olive had vague memories of attending those shows, of watching in awe as her mother became someone else, someone with a story to tell, some-one who could render an audience breathless. She vividly remembered her mother's final show, when years of belting it out finally took its toll on her voice. The strained, off-key performance was sensational in the worst possible way, an undignified end to an otherwise magnificent career.

Humiliated, Laurel had turned her attention to her daughter's career instead. After Olive's disastrous recital, Laurel took control of everything, booking auditions, preparing recital material, maintaining a careful practice regimen. Everything Olive did was under constant scrutiny, and for most of her life, she'd tried her hardest to win her mother's approval. A word or two of praise, and Olive would glow—but criticism always followed, like a bucket of icy water.

Eventually, Olive had come to realize that her mother wasn't trying to help her become the best singer she could be. She was trying to re-create her own career, but with a happier ending.

Olive did want to perform. But as herself, not as a mistake to be corrected. Which was why, in a small act of rebellion, Olive had chosen her own secret audition music. It was a song Laurel disapproved of and, therefore, Olive adored. In the final weeks of school, she'd caught herself humming the tune during classes; tangling the lyrics up with sonnet couplets in English; solving for x and getting B-flat in math. She practiced it whenever she was alone: in the tub; in her bed; on the balcony, where her voice was lost to the sounds of traffic below. She thought she was quite good, in all honesty. But practicing Mrs. Preiss's music was another story. There was no joy in singing if *she* was involved.

Olive did not have stage fright. It was more like mother fright.

Today, though, would be different. Because of the sheer number of children auditioning, family and friends were not allowed to watch the process. Olive felt a shiver of anticipation at the idea of standing on a stage and singing her own song, free from her mother's critical gaze. She *could* land a good role—maybe even a leading role.

She exhaled shakily as Mrs. Preiss swung the car into a parking space. Stepping outside, Olive closed her door and patted her hair self-consciously. *Hello, frizzies.* The thick, humid air filled her mouth and coated her throat like the bland lentil soup that had been last night's dinner.

Olive and her mother entered the lobby and joined the line of parents and children at the registration desk. Olive kept her eyes downcast, doing her best to ignore all the excited chatter. If anyone had tried to strike up a friendly conversation with her at that moment, they just might walk away with lentil soup on their sandals.

At the desk, Olive pulled her enrollment forms and piano sheet music out of her folder. Mrs. Preiss took them, lips pursed tight as she unclipped the check and handed it to a smiling woman. She squinted down at the forms, then up at Mrs. Preiss, and her face brightened.

"Preiss! Oh my goodness, you're Laurel Preiss, aren't you? *The* Laurel Preiss? *My Dearest Bernice* was the very first musical I ever saw—you were just incredible!"

Olive's mother forced a smile. "Thank you, that's very kind."

"Of course, you were Laurel Bernstein then," the woman continued chattering as she stamped and filed the forms. "You were, what, eleven or twelve years old? So incredible. And your daughter's auditioning for our little camp? How exciting! I bet your fa—"

The woman's face tightened for just a moment, and Olive looked down. She hated seeing the look on others' faces when they remembered what had happened to her father, and she silently prayed the topic would not come up.

"Well, anyway," the woman said, clearly flustered. "Good luck, sweetie—although I'm sure Laurel Preiss's daughter doesn't need luck."

She handed Olive a tag with an audition number—eighty—and pointed them to the backstage entrance down the corridor and to the right. Olive squeezed the tag, itching to get away from her mother. She hoped she could make it through the audition without everyone finding out she was Laurel Preiss's daughter. If Olive did well, she wanted to know it was due to her own talent.

"I know parents aren't allowed to watch the auditions,"

Mrs. Preiss said crisply. "But I was wondering if you might make an exception for me." Olive's head snapped up, dread seeping into her stomach like cement.

The woman's eyes widened. "Oh, of course!" She glanced around, then lowered her voice to a conspiratorial whisper. "Come back here after you take your daughter backstage, and I'll sneak you in." She winked, clearly pleased with herself, and was rewarded with another thin-lipped smile.

"Thank you."

Mrs. Preiss took Olive's arm and led her down the hall before the woman could gush any further. Olive was in shock. Months of preparation, wasted. Now she couldn't sing her song. She had to sing the one her mother had chosen, the way she had taught Olive to sing it. As always.

Years ago, Olive had found the clipping of a musical review published the year before she was born, tucked away in her mother's makeup drawer.

With her striking beauty and powerful voice, it's no surprise Laurel Preiss steals our hearts with every leading role she takes on. But there are moments when we catch a glimpse of something else—a coy look with a hint of menace; sweet words laced with a steely edge— and we can't help but wonder if her talents might be better harnessed in a different role. As enchanting as her heroines are, imagine the delicious wickedness Laurel Preiss might unleash as a villain.

Olive had once been naïve enough to laugh at the very idea.

They stopped at the backstage entrance, and Mrs. Preiss turned to her daughter with hypercritical eyes.

"Smile," she said sharply, adjusting Olive's barrette again. "No, wider. There. If you walk out on that stage with a droopy face, your audition will be over before it begins."

Olive nodded, her cheeks already aching.

"We should have gone with the blue dress," Mrs. Preiss murmured, pinning the audition tag to Olive's blouse. "This outfit's a bit too . . . conservative." She glanced at Olive's face, eyes narrowing. "You look pale. Are you feeling sick again?"

"No," Olive lied. A pounding had begun behind her temples.

Pulling the backstage door open, Mrs. Preiss gestured for Olive to enter. "I'll be waiting in the lobby afterward. And, Olive?"

"Yes?" Once upon a time, this was the moment her mother would soften just a bit. A quick kiss on the fore-head, or a small smile and a whispered *You'll be fine.* Olive stared up at her mother, a tiny ember of hope sparking in her chest.

"Check your posture. You've been slouching lately."

The ember fizzled out with a *hiss.*

Squaring her shoulders, Olive nodded and smiled wide,

wide, wide. She waited until the door clicked closed before sticking her tongue out.

She wanted to scream, or kick something, or cry in frustration. But dozens of children huddled in clusters backstage, and several more were scattered around, mouthing lyrics or singing warm-ups. So Olive stuck to the wall near a rack of costumes, scanning each face and trying to breathe normally. She didn't recognize anyone from school, which was good. Interacting with other children came with its own kind of performance anxiety these days.

It hadn't always been this way. Elementary school was simple enough: Olive had friends to play hopscotch with at recess, and one or two "enemies" who poked fun at the contents of her packed lunch. But her first year of middle school had been different. Olive no longer had friends or enemies. She didn't want either. She simply existed, a ghost of a girl moving from class to class.

She moved that way now, slipping around the costume rack, avoiding eye contact with anyone who looked overly friendly. She peered through the curtains and saw a teenage boy standing center stage. A few adults sat in the front row, and Olive immediately recognized a red-haired woman as the theater camp director from her photo in the brochure. Children who had already auditioned were laughing and chatting in groups throughout the auditorium. Olive imagined her mother in the crowd, and her stomach clenched.

"Number fifty-two, Ernie Smith . . . ready?"

The boy gave a little salute, and the director smiled. She gestured to the pianist in the orchestra pit, a young man with heavy-lidded eyes who looked as though he needed a few extra hours of sleep. As the opening chords sounded, Olive backed away from the curtains. She hurried to a quiet, dark corner and sank to the floor next to an oversize wardrobe. A prop, she thought distantly, tracing a finger over the painted wood. She decided to distract herself by focusing on the show rather than the audition and her mother's presence.

Olive loved that moment when the house lights dimmed and the curtain rose and the audience saw not actors in costumes surrounded by set pieces, but living, breathing characters in a whole different world. She wanted desperately to be a part of that. To walk onto a stage and become someone else entirely. But how could she become someone else, someone *better,* when her mother was always there to point out her flaws?

"Number fifty-three?"

Olive's heart thumped extrahard. Leaning against the wardrobe, she closed her eyes and tried to master herself. So what if her mother was watching? Olive might never be good enough for Mrs. Preiss, but she could be good enough for theater camp. She could march out on that stage and tell the pianist not to bother with the sheet music, because she would be singing a cappella.

And then she would sing *her* song. Perhaps she'd impress

the director or even catch the eye of a talent scout. Starring roles in major productions, taking the stage at the city's most illustrious theaters, fame and fortune . . . that could be Olive's destiny. And she didn't have to follow the path her mother had laid out to get there.

The thought filled Olive with hope. But each time the director called the next audition number, the knot in her stomach tightened. At fifty-eight, her hands started to shake. At sixty-six, her pulse thrummed in her ears. At seventy-nine, Olive seriously considered just hiding in the wardrobe for the entirety of the camp. And then . . .

"Number eighty?"

Somehow, Olive stood. She headed onto the stage with an odd feeling of detachment. The red-haired director beamed up at her.

"Olive?"

"Yes."

"Olive *Preiss*?" A few heads looked up at this emphasis on her last name, and Olive silently willed the director not to say anything about her mother.

"Yes." Suddenly, Olive realized she wasn't smiling. Panicking, she compensated by grinning so hard her cheeks stung. In the fourth row, a few girls giggled. The director shot them a warning look over her shoulder before turning back to Olive.

"Okay, then!" she said cheerfully. "Here we go. . . ."

The pianist, yawning widely, nodded. Olive opened her

mouth to tell them she'd changed her selection. But against her will, her eyes darted around the auditorium until they fell on a lone figure standing in the back, half hidden in shadow. Olive could feel her mother's gaze locked on her. The opening chords to the song Mrs. Preiss had selected sounded.

Olive didn't even inhale. Bright spots danced in front of her eyes as her cue came and went.

Looking concerned, the director waved at the pianist to stop. "Are you okay, Olive?"

No, Olive wanted to scream. But her head moved up and down like a puppet's instead.

"Shall we try again?"

Nod, nod, nod. Olive heard a few more muffled giggles, saw her mother take a step forward. She felt feverish under the lights, her starchy blouse and skirt scratching her skin. The pianist plunked out the opening chords once more, and Olive felt the sudden urge to scream, *That's not my song!*

At the cue, she drew a breath. But the first line came out shrill, and her voice cracked on the second. She trailed off to more laughter, tears burning her eyes.

The director twisted around in her seat, scowling and hushing the others. When she turned back, Olive had already fled the stage.

3

That Lovely Audition

The sky hung low and gray as Olive sprinted from the arts center, past the poster-covered bus stop, and down the street. She slowed after two blocks, wiping her eyes. The humidity settled on her skin and coated her lungs as she made her way deeper into the theater district. With each street she crossed, the advertisements grew larger, flashier, brighter. They weren't all for musicals, though most were. Or maybe Olive's eyes just found those faster. Despite bad times, people were still willing to spend some of their hard-earned money on entertainment. They were just pickier now, and theaters fought for their attention with increasingly desperate promises of glitz and glamour.

Excited tourists and harried locals bustled around her, a cacophony of snapping cameras, jabbing elbows, and muttered obscenities. The distant rumble of thunder did little to thin out the crowd. Olive wandered aimlessly, shoulders hunched, head down as if the storm had already begun. A fat drop splashed against her arm, then her cheek. Turning off onto a smaller, quieter street, Olive peered around for a place to hide, maybe a bookshop or café. Her gaze fell on a marquee that read:

MAUDEVILLE

Another warm drop of water trickled down Olive's forehead as she approached the theater. It wasn't particularly large, as the city's theaters went. Old but elegant, with a grand staircase, thick granite columns, and a mosaic of greens, blues, and browns adorning the facade like jewels. It glimmered enticingly. Perhaps this was one of the few places left still untouched by hard times.

One of the thick double doors stood slightly ajar. The rainfall increased from sporadic to steady, and Olive made up her mind. She hurried up the steps and pulled the doors open. The downpour began with a crash of thunder the moment she stepped inside.

Olive closed the doors, the *click* echoing off the black-and-white marble floor. She glanced around the empty lobby nervously. It was larger than she'd expected; not so much in width but in length, stretching back to another set of grand double doors to the auditorium. Wrought-iron chandeliers hung overhead, draped with . . . cobwebs?

Olive's stomach gave an unpleasant lurch. Squinting harder, she realized they were actually delicate strands of shimmering crystals, and she laughed a little at her mistake.

"Hello?" she called, taking a few hesitant steps. No one answered. Monday, Olive realized: most theaters were closed on Mondays. But the doors had been open. Surely someone was here.

When she passed the first of several stately white columns, Olive gasped. A large portrait hung on the wall to her right—a woman with dark curls and wide, glittering eyes, glancing coyly over her bare shoulder. Her lipsticked lips were curved in a small smile, but most of her face was hidden in shadow.

Olive gazed at her for a moment, then continued forward. Different portraits of the same glamorous woman lined the walls between the columns. When Olive reached the doors to the auditorium, she glanced at the portrait on her left. The woman's head was tilted back in easy laughter, her eyes dancing with mirth.

A lightness filled Olive for the first time that day. She pulled the doors open and let out a small cry of astonishment.

It wasn't the largest hall she'd ever seen, but it was by far the most beautiful. The seats and curtains were a rich plum, the candelabras and railings bronze. The high, domed ceiling featured intricate carvings that, from this distance, formed a pattern resembling feathery wings.

Many of the city's theaters had begun to look rundown, and a few had even closed permanently. But this, this looked the way all theaters had looked to Olive back when money was unlimited, when everything was lavish and luxurious and easy and everyone believed life would be this way forever and ever.

Olive wandered down the aisle, brushing her fingers along the backs of the chairs and stirring up flurries of dust particles that sparkled in the soft light emanating from a lamp on the stage. She heard the muffled, distant sound of the thunderstorm, steady rainfall punctuated by the occasional rumble or whisper. . . .

Freezing, Olive glanced around the empty hall. She'd heard someone whisper; she was sure of it. Her eyes searched every corner before she continued, more cautiously now, toward the front.

The orchestra pit contained a few chairs and an old upright piano, sheet music stacked neatly on top. Olive began climbing the steps to the stage, tripping when the pages rustled. She spun around and caught a glimpse of something—a flutter of movement accompanied by the scuttling sound of a feather-light spider. And now a single sheet of music stood at the ready, leaning against the rack over the piano keys.

Olive blinked, casting a wary eye around the hall again before stepping onto the stage and walking to the center. Taking a deep breath, she faced the empty hall and imagined every seat filled. This was a stage on which one could become someone else, a character in a different, better world.

The silence felt larger than the theater itself—even the storm outside had quieted. Yet still, there was a sense of

anticipation here, one Olive thought must be inherent to any performance hall. The feeling that a collective breath was being held, waiting for the first note.

Without thinking about it, as if she'd meant to do it all along, Olive began to sing.

The lyrics, *her* lyrics, spilled out effortlessly. Her voice filled the hall, spreading out past every row and up into the balconies until it reached every corner. By the time the last note escaped her, Olive was beaming and breathless. She listened to the echo of her own voice fade somewhere up in the domed ceiling. This was the happiest she'd felt in almost a year.

Then a shadow stirred in the far left corner of the hall, and fear seized her by the throat.

Somehow, her mother had found her.

Olive's mind reeled for an explanation, an apology. But when the figure moved down the aisle into the light, words failed her completely. This was most definitely *not* her mother.

The beautiful woman from the portraits stood in the aisle, dark and elegant. She was tall, very tall, and her crimson lips were curved in the widest smile Olive had ever seen.

"Thank you for that lovely audition, darling," she said, her voice low and throaty. "I believe I have just the part for you."

4
A Worthy Replacement

Olive gaped at the woman. "A-audition?" she stammered, the word round and clumsy in her mouth. "I wasn't auditioning."

The woman arched a black eyebrow. "Weren't you?" she asked pleasantly. "Forgive me. When someone stands on my stage and offers the perfect song, I suppose it's only natural for me to assume she wants a part in my show."

The perfect song.

Flushed, Olive squeezed her hands to stop her fingers from trembling. "I didn't mean to . . . it was raining, and . . ." She tried to swallow it back, but the question burst out. "You thought that was perfect?"

The smile grew wider. "Perfect for you, of course. I'm Maude Devore, my dear. May I ask your name?"

"Olive Preiss."

"Hello, Olive Preiss." Maude began climbing the stairs, and Olive heard another flurry of whispers. Startled, she glanced out at the empty seats. When she turned back, the woman loomed over her. Olive inhaled shakily, the warm scent of flowers and fresh dirt tickling her nostrils.

Just as in her portraits, Maude Devore was all paint and powder: liquid black hair piled high on her head, with a few soft, loose curls contrasting her scalpel-slash cheek-bones; shimmering chartreuse swiped beneath arched, penciled brows; and the reddest lipstick imaginable, which made her broad mouth appear broader and her many, many teeth shine whiter.

"If you weren't auditioning for my show," Maude said, brushing a speck of dust off her skirt with a casual flick, "may I ask what brought you here?"

Olive's mouth opened and closed. She was here to wait out the storm . . . but of course, there was more. Much more. The whole story spilled out before Olive could stop herself: her controlling, critical mother; the disastrous audition; fleeing in humiliation.

"I'm so sorry I just walked in like this," Olive finished breathlessly. "I didn't mean to come up here and start sing-ing. It just . . . happened."

"Of course it did," Maude agreed. "Because you, Olive, are a performer. That is what we do." She stepped closer, and Olive caught another whiff of garden scent. It reminded her of the pot of red chrysanthemums her father used to keep on the desk in his study. "Regardless of what brought you here, my offer stands," Maude said. "As it happens, my show stars a child. And you, darling, are absolutely perfect for the role."

Olive swayed slightly. "Me?"

"You." Maude smiled again. "I'm in a bit of a tight spot, you see, and I think we might be able to help each other out. My former star moved on rather unexpectedly, and I haven't been able to find a worthy replacement. If you were to take on that role, I—and my cast—would be so grateful. And I would be happy to keep your participation a secret, at least for now. Your mother doesn't need to know." Maude gestured to the empty chairs. "Until opening night, of course."

Staring at the auditorium, Olive imagined a packed house, all eyes on her.

"We can invite her if you wish," Maude whispered. "And she'll see how magnificent you really are."

Olive's head felt fuzzy. This was entirely too easy. No one, absolutely no one, simply walked into a theater to be handed a role—a *starring* role. But standing in this beautiful hall, flushed from finally having sung her song and basking in praise she never heard at home, Olive felt herself nodding in agreement.

"Okay."

Maude's lips curved up once more.

"Wonderful."

Turning, she glided across the stage toward the stairs,

and Olive hurried after her. Maude continued talking as they made their way back to the lobby, but Olive hardly heard a word. She followed in a daze until a flutter against her elbow caused her to jump in fright.

Olive spun in a circle, staring wildly around the lobby. Something had fallen near her feet: a coil of measuring tape.

"Ah, I apologize." Maude sounded amused. "My seamstresses are getting ahead of themselves, taking your measurements already."

"Seamstresses?" Olive repeated. "Where? I didn't see anyone."

"As is often the case with ghosts." Maude laughed at Olive's expression. "Come now, darling. Every theater has its ghosts—surely you know that by now."

Olive did know. Most theaters in the city were rumored to be haunted—and everyone knew that the more ghosts a theater had, the better its reputation. After all, nothing attested to the quality of a performance hall more than the refusal of its artists to depart it, even in death. The Alcazar, where Mrs. Preiss had often performed, famously saved a single seat at every show for the ghost of its very first producer. Several theaters were known to light candles backstage to ward off malevolent spirits of former actors who might steal the show from the living. Olive had a clear memory of actually seeing a ghost onstage once, when she was seven and her parents had season tickets to Crescent Court Theater. A man in a pinstripe suit who had most certainly not been in the show had nonetheless taken a bow during curtain call with the cast—then vanished. Olive's parents hadn't noticed, but Olive heard the couple behind them whispering about the apparition. Apparently, he was the ghost of a well-known actor who'd performed at the theater decades earlier until a tragic prop mishap resulted in his rather dramatic onstage demise.

But Olive had never had such a close encounter before. She cast another nervous glance around the lobby, rubbing the spot where the measuring tape had grazed her elbow. "Are they nice?" she asked timidly. "The ghosts?"

"Oh, very," Maude answered. "I wouldn't allow them to stay otherwise."

They reached the doors, and Maude smiled down at Olive.

"I'll see you tomorrow, then?"

A tingling spread through Olive's chest, and she nodded. "Yes. And thank you!"

Olive yanked the doors open and then hurried down the steps. The rain had slowed to a drizzle, silver light shining along the edge of the clouds. Olive floated through the streets like a helium balloon, filled to bursting with happiness. Forget theater camp—she was going to be part of a *real* show. In a haunted theater, no less. And her mother had no idea.

Olive made her way back through the theater district with Maude's Cheshire Cat smile still dancing in her vision.

5

Hollow Home

The parking space was empty.

Confused, Olive gazed at the spot where her mother had parked the car. Maude's encouraging words had rung in her ears the whole walk back to the arts center. But as the fog of Maudeville lifted, realization began to dawn. Over an hour had passed since Olive had fled her audition without a word to anyone. And now Mrs. Preiss was gone.

Squinting at the arts center's entrance, Olive wondered if she should ask someone inside for help. Auditions were still going on, after all. She imagined slinking back in, the daughter of one of the city's theater legends, who couldn't even get through an audition—the whispers, the stares, the laughter. . . .

Olive hesitated, wiping her sweaty palms on her skirt. Then she turned away from the center. She didn't have money for the bus, but she could walk home. It wasn't too far.

The hot midafternoon sun beat down on her as she trudged block after block. Her damp hair stuck to her forehead, sweat causing her starchy blouse to cling to her skin as if magnetized. Olive breathed a sigh of relief when she finally saw the city's oldest library up ahead. The stately gray building sat on the outskirts of the historic district—a left turn and three more blocks, and she'd be home.

When Olive turned onto her street at last, the sight of a police car parked in front of her building sent a chill through her despite the heat.

Steeling herself, Olive marched past the Marinos' coffee shop and into her building. To her relief, the doorman was nowhere to be seen. Olive glanced at the numbers over the elevator doors just as the dial moved from seven to six. Quickly, she hurried to the stairs and began the climb to the ninth-floor penthouse.

At the top, out of breath, Olive pulled her key from her pocket. But the door swung open just before she reached it. A tall, thin policeman nearly barreled into her, blinked in confusion for a few seconds, then hollered over his shoulder: "The girl's right here!"

The next hour passed in a nightmarish blur. Olive answered question after question, perched stiffly on the edge of the sofa. She'd left the arts center and wandered around the theater district. No, she hadn't spoken to any strangers. No, she hadn't thought to call home from a pay phone. No, she hadn't given her actions much thought at all. She did not say a word about Maudeville—now was not the time, not with her mother's fingers gripping her shoulder like talons.

Mrs. Preiss had appeared genuinely shocked—maybe even relieved—upon seeing Olive in the doorway. What followed was a commendable performance: fluttering hands, trembling smiles, soothing murmurings. But while the police officers failed to detect the underlying current of ire in her mother's voice, Olive did not. And when the pair finally took their leave, Olive braced herself for the worst.

She sat rigid, hands clasped in her lap as her mother said goodbye to the officers at the door. Directly across the room, the wallpaper bore a dark patch, perfectly rectangular in shape. It took Olive a moment to remember. A painting had hung there: a still lake beneath a fiery sky. The bronze frame had been quite expensive. It had hung right there on the wall all of Olive's life, and now it was gone.

When Mr. Preiss died last summer, he'd taken the family's source of income with him. The penthouse was paid off, but gas, electricity, and food bills piled up quickly. Not to mention paychecks for the house staff. Her mother seemed determined that her husband's abrupt departure would not put an end to their lifestyle. And as she reminded Olive frequently, Mrs. Preiss herself was unsuited to any work outside of performing. So another means of income was necessary.

It had begun with the gold angel bookends. One day, they proudly guarded the second-to-top row of books on Olive's shelf—her mysteries, her darkest and most treasured stories, the ones her father had read aloud to her when she was little. The next day, they were gone, swapped for enough money to keep the heat on all winter. The mere memory was enough to fill Olive with fury.

The love seat had been the second to go, bringing in a few weeks' worth of groceries. The grandfather clock followed, covering the last of Olive's tuition payments for the year. And so it had continued as the weather grew warmer, a sad sort of spring-cleaning. Eventually, Mrs. Preiss had been forced to let the house staff go anyway. Now it was just the two of them, Olive and her mother, alone together in their increasingly hollow home.

"So."

Olive forced herself to look up. Her mother glared down at her, dark eyes cold and hard. There was no tenderness there now, no relief—that had all been an act for the police officers. And a very good act at that.

Imagine the delicious wickedness Laurel Preiss might unleash as a villain. When she'd first read that review, Olive found the idea of her mother as a villain amusing. But right now, those words tugged at a carefully stitched-up hole in her chest, and Olive feared it might unravel completely.

"Stand up."

Olive obeyed, legs shaking. Mrs. Preiss stood quite still.

"It's not just the money you've thrown away in spite of our . . . situation." Her voice, cold and low, grew louder with every word. "It's not just the fact that you stood on that stage and didn't even try, didn't even *bother,* after all the work we've put in the last few months. It's not just that I had to call the police, that the entire building saw them come here to question me, like a criminal. That would be bad enough, but you . . ." Mrs. Preiss paused, drew a deep breath. Her arms hung loose at her sides, shoulders low, chin high—the seemingly relaxed stance of a singer preparing to belt it out.

"You ran away."

Olive looked at her feet.

"You ran away," Mrs. Preiss repeated, and now there was a subtle shift in her tone. Disbelief. Olive had never dared defy her mother. "You just took off into the city without a thought of what might happen. What it would put me through. What people will say, as if we needed to give them any more reason to—" She stopped abruptly, jaw clenching and unclenching. "What were you *thinking,* Olive?" she spat. "We prepared for this. You were ready. You can't just up and vanish when things get difficult; that's not how life works."

"It worked for Dad."

A long moment passed before Olive realized, with a thrill of horror, that those words had actually come from her mouth. The look of shock on her mother's face mirrored Olive's own. A second later, she gasped at the sharp sting of a hand across her face.

Laurel Preiss glared down at her daughter, eyes wild and wide. "Your room. Now."

Olive did not hesitate. She fled the living room, hurrying down the hall, past the door to her father's study. She climbed onto her four-post bed and lay on top of the covers. Closing her eyes, Olive imagined a glowing-red handprint on her cheek. She fell asleep long before it faded away.

•

6

The Fire Escape

Olive awoke with a buzzing headache and a general sense of doom. She lay in bed blinking away her dream, in which she'd soared over a grand stage, chased by a relentless spotlight. At last, she got dressed and headed to the kitchen. A curt note waited next to a bowl of cold oatmeal.

I've notified the doorman that you are not to leave the building. I'll be home before dinner.
— Mother

Sighing, Olive picked up her spoon. A hint of Mrs. Preiss's spicy perfume lingered in the air; judging from the dirty dishes stacked next to the sink, she'd left in a hurry. Olive took a bite of oatmeal, gazing at the red lipstick smiling at her from the rim of one of the coffee cups. Then she promptly choked.

Maudeville. It hadn't been a dream. Hurrying to the sink, Olive filled a clean glass with water and took a long sip.

Maude Devore had offered her a starring role, and Olive had promised to return to the theater today. Which would be difficult to do, thanks to her mother.

Olive left the kitchen, thinking hard. Perhaps there was some way she could disguise herself to sneak past the doorman and escape.

Escape.

Suddenly, Olive knew exactly what she needed to do.

In a dim corner of her mind, she realized she was about to defy her mother again. The second time in as many days. The thought gave her a thrill. Where this sudden rebellious streak had come from, Olive wasn't sure. *It worked for Dad.* Olive could not have wielded a weapon sharper than those words. She pictured her mother's expression and felt a wave of guilt. And maybe just the tiniest hint of satisfaction.

And now she stood in front of her father's study.

Lifting her chin, Olive reached for the doorknob. Neither she nor her mother had entered the study since last summer. Mrs. Preiss had closed the door a week after her husband's funeral, and by some unspoken mother-daughter agreement, it had remained shut. Olive had longed to enter more than once, but she knew it was best to stay out. It had taken her a long time to stitch up the hole that had ripped open in her chest when her father died, and she didn't want to undo that work. But maybe enough time had passed.

Olive pushed the door open.

Clutter. Beautiful, glorious clutter—shelves crammed

with books and knickknacks; papers and photos and pens covering the surface of the sturdy rosewood desk; filing cabinets so stuffed with documents, the drawers couldn't close properly. Olive smiled at the familiar sight, though her throat ached. Compared to her father's wonderfully messy haven, the rest of the penthouse seemed even emptier. She stepped inside and closed the door behind her.

Directly across the room, a sheet was draped over the mirror. The stout desk sat in front of it, with bookshelves lining the wall to the right. And of course, the silver telescope on its stout tripod, right next to the window. The curtains were parted, offering a glimpse of the short red-brick building across the alley. This mostly unobstructed view of the sky had prompted Mr. Preiss to buy the telescope. It was a rather extravagant purchase made after money had begun rapidly drying up, and Mrs. Preiss had made her disapproval clear. But Mr. Preiss had insisted that they needed this splurge now more than ever, to lift their spirits.

On clear nights, Olive and her father would take turns stargazing while Mrs. Preiss sat in the plush leather armchair behind the desk with a cup of tea. Mr. Preiss would point out all sorts of constellations and tell Olive stories to go with the pictures they formed—tales of snakes wrapped around chariots, or boastful queens and noble centaurs. Inevitably, he would begin inventing new constellations, and Mrs. Preiss would halfheartedly protest.

"Stick to the real constellations," she'd say. "The ones Olive needs to know for school."

"The *real* ones?" Mr. Preiss would laugh. "They're all made up, aren't they?" His wife would roll her eyes as Olive and her father shared a grin. "Infinite stars mean infinite constellations, Olive," he'd say. "They can show any picture, tell any story that you want to see. They're all made up, and they're all real."

Olive hadn't stargazed in more than a year.

She walked over to the plush leather chair behind the desk and, after a moment's hesitation, sat. Hands clasped in her lap, she surveyed the mess. Her father was one of those people who had a method of organization all their own. Several dusty books were piled in the corner, all with worn covers and laborious-sounding titles. A calendar lay beneath a few open notebooks filled with scrawling, sloppy penmanship. Some plastic pill bottles with prescription labels sat next to a coffee mug that read *History Haunts Us*. Everything looked in disarray, but ask Mr. Preiss for a specific book or a certain letter, and he'd have it in hand within seconds.

A large map took up much of his workspace. Examining the streets, Olive realized it was a map of the historic district. As a historian, Mr. Preiss had a particular passion for his city's past. Olive gazed at the map, the streets nothing but meaningless squiggles. She had come here because she needed to escape without the doorman noticing. But she was having second thoughts.

Not about sneaking out. Just about doing it this way.

Exhaling slowly, Olive stood, pushed the chair back to the desk, and headed to the window. It let out the softest of creaks when she yanked it open. Without allowing herself even a second to reconsider, Olive put one leg through, then the other, taking care not to kick the telescope. A moment later, she stood on the fire escape, gripping the railing and staring at the ground below.

Nine floors down. And no one around to see.

Olive began the descent down the ladder. On the sixth floor, Ms. Asher's shih tzu, Tinkerbell, began yapping so loudly that Olive twitched in surprise. By the third floor, her hands were slick with sweat and she nearly slipped off. But soon she hung from the very last rung, legs swaying for a few seconds before she let go. Her feet hit the pavement with a *smack*.

Standing, Olive brushed off her legs and cast a quick glance around. A couple strolled hand in hand across the street, and an elderly woman left the Marinos' coffee shop on the corner carrying a cake box. None of them noticed the sweaty, shaky girl next to the garbage cans.

Olive crept to the edge of the alley and peeked in the coffee shop window to make sure Mrs. Marino wasn't watching. Then she sprinted off in the direction of the theater district as fast as her legs could take her.

7

A Sudden, Particular Kind of Hope

Olive ran past the library where her father used to work. She ran past the arts center, where theater camp would soon begin. She ran past the parking lot and the bus stops covered in posters and the buildings that gradually swelled in size, retracing her steps from yesterday until she couldn't run any longer.

Rubbing at a stitch in her side, Olive turned in a slow circle. Had she passed that billboard yesterday, the cologne advertisement with an image of a cowboy lassoing a horse? And that cabaret club up ahead—she'd turned left on the street before it, hadn't she? Or maybe it was the next street over. . . .

A man in a suit skirted around her, black coffee splashing over the rim of the paper cup in his hand. He muttered a rude word, which Olive ignored. She was too busy fighting down her panic. The arcade with all the pinball machines lined up out front—she'd walked past that yesterday for sure. Then she'd crossed this intersection. . . . No, it was a right turn, past the great, glittering Alcazar theater, then a turn onto this narrow street, and—

Olive's heart soared at the sight of a familiar marquee. She'd nearly reached the stairs when a voice behind her piped up.

"You're not going in there, are you?"

Whirling around, Olive stared at the boy leaning against the dumpster in the alley. He was maybe a year or so older than she was, with unkempt black hair and ragged, stained clothes. He regarded her with a cool yet suspicious expression, which Olive instinctively mirrored.

"So what if I am?"

A rat scurried out from under the dumpster, darting around the boy's feet. He didn't flinch. "Have you been in there before?"

"Yes. Yesterday."

He squinted at her. "What did it look like?"

"Look like?" Olive repeated, wrinkling her nose. "It looks like a theater. It's lovely."

The boy's face fell. Olive took another step up the stairs, then another. She was itching to find Maude and prove to the tiny nagging voice in her head that yesterday had not, in fact, been a dream. The boy watched warily as she pulled the doors open, but he said nothing when she slipped inside.

The lobby was just as Olive remembered. Beaming, she hurried past the columns and portraits toward the hall.

When she tugged on the door handles, her heart sank. The auditorium was locked.

Olive pressed her ear against the door, but all was quiet within. Frustrated and slightly panicky, Olive turned around and found herself face to face with an extremely pale ghost.

"Oh!" she cried, leaning back against the doors. The ghost tilted his head, regarding her curiously. Blinking, Olive realized he wasn't transparent. Not a ghost, then.

He was, however, a mime.

His head and neck were covered in white paint. His eyelids and lips were an inky black, complemented by a black spade on his right cheek and a red heart on his left. A single black teardrop glistened at the corner of his left eye. He wore a black beret over his shaved-bald head, along with a long-sleeved shirt with black-and-white prisoner stripes, white gloves, black pants, and shiny black shoes. Bright red suspenders added the only other touch of color to his look.

"Hello," Olive breathed. The mime smiled kindly at her, and she relaxed a bit. "Is . . . is Maude here?" He pointed down the hallway to the right, then mimed walking up steps. Olive giggled nervously. "She's upstairs?" Nodding, he offered his elbow with an exaggeratedly chivalrous gesture. Olive hesitated, then took his arm and allowed him to lead her down the hall. It dead-ended at a door, which the mime pushed open to reveal a staircase.

Olive kept sneaking glances at him as they climbed

the stairs. It was difficult to judge his age, thanks to all the makeup. His face was smooth save for a few wrinkles around his eyes, which were the warm shade of maple syrup. The mime caught her staring and winked.

"What's your name?" she asked. He stopped abruptly on the landing and let go of her arm. For a moment, Olive feared she had offended him. Then he broke into a wild tap dance, legs flailing in a way that at first appeared clumsy but that Olive soon realized possessed a controlled, fluid grace. He finished with a flourish, holding his arms out with a beseeching expression.

"You're named after a tap dancer?" Olive asked, and the mime nodded eagerly. "Okay . . . I think I need another hint."

Standing straight and tall, the mime removed his beret and pretended to put his arm through it before placing it on his bald head. He held his palms flat and parallel above the beret, moving his hands up and down to indicate length. "A top hat?" Olive guessed, and he beamed. Then he pulled on his ears so that they stuck out, and he did a few more tap moves. Olive snickered. "Sorry, but I've still got no idea."

He let out a melodramatic sigh, then smiled and shrugged. Still laughing, Olive followed him up the rest of the stairs.

The mime led her down a dim corridor and past a door that stood slightly ajar. Olive peeked inside; the blue-tiled floor was covered in long tables and benches. Noticing her curious look, the mime pretended to fork food into his mouth, rubbing his belly and smiling.

Olive grinned. "Kitchen?" The mime nodded happily.

They continued in this fashion, stopping in front of each door for a short pantomime explanation of the room. Olive was surprised to find the theater had a dormitory—one rather large room crammed with cots and bunk beds. Just down the corridor was the bathroom (here, the mime's scrunched-up expression as he squatted gave Olive an uncontrollable case of the giggles). At last, they rounded the corner and Olive saw that the hall dead-ended at a set of double doors. The mime bounded ahead, pushing them open with a grandiose air. Olive stepped inside and gasped.

At first glance, the room appeared infinitely large and filled with countless people. But Olive quickly realized that was just a trick of the mirrored walls. Even so, it was quite spacious, with dark hardwood floors and a high ceiling. She'd barely taken a scan of the people scattered around the room—juggling, making cards vanish, breathing fire—before the mime stepped in front of her. Clearing his throat, he lifted an imaginary megaphone to his mouth and pretended to shout.

To Olive's astonishment, all heads swiveled in their direction as if the people had heard him. And then the cast of Maudeville descended upon her, wringing her hand and patting her on the back. Olive smiled and attempted to look confident, though her knees wobbled a bit.

The juggler—a teenage black girl named Tanisha, with a shy smile and a short, tight braid—reached out to shake Olive's hand. She was promptly elbowed in the head by an impossibly muscular guy with spiky, bright red hair that contrasted sharply with his pale face. He apologized to Tanisha profusely before introducing himself to Olive as Mickey—the fire-eater, judging by the torch swinging at his side. Next came Valentine the magician, a young woman—or a young man? Olive wasn't quite sure—with light brown skin, straight black hair that fell to his (or her) shoulders, and a red button-down shirt with a pattern of winking eyes. Eli the aerialist followed, a petite blond man with a neatly trimmed beard and round, rosy cheeks. Though he was the shortest of the group, Olive thought he looked the oldest, maybe in his upper twenties.

The youngest stepped forward last. Olive's spine stiffened instinctively at the sight of a girl around her own age. "My assistant, Juliana," Valentine told Olive, who attempted a polite but indifferent smile. "Most talented girl I've ever sawed in half." Juliana grinned at the floor, toying with her long, dark ponytail.

"Hang on—where're Aidan and Nadia?" Mickey squinted around the rehearsal space, twirling his torch absent-mindedly.

"Costume malfunction, I think. They're with the seamstresses." Tanisha smiled at Olive. "You still haven't told us your name!"

"Oh, I'm sorry!" Olive felt her face heat up. "I'm—"

But the mime stepped forward again, clearing his throat. Nose in the air, he stirred an imaginary drink before taking a sip with a haughty expression.

Mickey was the first to guess. "Martini?"

Giving him an exasperated look, the mime pretended to fish something out of the drink. He waved it at Mickey before popping it into his mouth. Mickey's brow furrowed. "Wait . . . your name's Onion?" he wondered, and Tanisha hid a grin behind her hand.

"I think *Olive* might suit her better," Eli said with a wink, and Olive nodded.

"That's right."

"Are you going to be in the show with us, Olive?" Valentine asked.

A familiar throaty voice behind Olive responded first.

"She's going to star in it."

Olive spun around to find Maude Devore behind her, smiling as broadly as ever. She felt a rush of pride as Maude moved to stand next to her. The other cast members stood up a little straighter, and Mickey's torch fell still at his side.

"Olive had an impromptu audition yesterday," Maude continued, winking at Olive. "We'll be working on her part in private today—full-cast rehearsals will begin next week. But believe me, Olive is just what we've been looking for since Finley's unfortunate departure."

The shift was immediate. A somber mood descended

like fog, and everyone nodded solemnly. Olive noticed that Juliana was blinking rapidly, eyes downcast, and an uneasy feeling of recognition settled over her. The girl's expression reflected a certain type of sadness with which Olive was well acquainted. Juliana caught her staring and, after a moment, gave her a small smile, which Olive returned.

A sudden, particular kind of hope took root in the pit of her stomach, one Olive hadn't felt in a long time. It was the magical feeling that happens when you see a bit of yourself in someone else and realize this might just be a person who will make you laugh and comfort you and keep your secrets. Even the deepest, darkest ones.

Olive looked away quickly. Ever since her father died last summer, she had been friendless by choice. The fewer people you loved, the less chance you would be abandoned.

So she just listened as Maude continued to discuss the upcoming rehearsals. And she tried not to notice the way Tanisha slipped a comforting arm around Juliana, how Mickey offered her a (slightly scorched) handkerchief, how Valentine and Eli pressed closer together, shoulders touching. She tried not to notice that they looked like a grieving family, because she was an outsider, and grief was a private thing.

But Olive couldn't help wondering what exactly had happened to the star she was replacing.

8
Eidola

Maude Devore's private studio was like the woman herself—beautiful and imposing. Olive perched nervously on the edge of a high-backed chair facing a mahogany desk even wider than her father's. Another chandelier hung overhead, slightly smaller than those in the lobby, but with seemingly twice the number of delicate, shimmering crystal strands. The thick velvety rug beneath Olive's feet was woven in a pattern of turquoise, black, and gold similar to the mosaic outside the theater, and a grand piano sat in the corner. A large black-and-white photograph hung on the wall behind the desk, featuring a dark-haired woman standing in the spotlight on a stage, head bowed. The photo was taken from a distance—the highest balcony, Olive thought—and all the seats below were filled.

"My final performance," Maude told her. "This was years and years ago, back when this theater had a different name. There was a fire that night, a terrible tragedy."

Olive's heart stuttered. "After the show?"

"During," Maude said sadly. "It started backstage and spread so quickly. . . . I took refuge in the trap room beneath the stage. But the rest of the cast, and the audience . . ." She paused, shaking her head. "It was a packed house, and there were too few exits. With all the panic, very few made it out alive."

"How horrible," Olive breathed, staring at the photo again. She tried to imagine the chaos and shuddered.

"Indeed," Maude agreed. "The auditorium was nearly destroyed, and the theater was closed for many years after that. But that's its own tragedy, isn't it? A hollow theater, an empty stage with no one to bring its stories to life. But a lowered curtain isn't content to remain that way forever, Olive. It's just waiting to rise again."

Her dark eyes locked onto Olive's and wouldn't let go.

"So I opened its doors once more. And now it's home to the most incredible show in the city. In my humble opinion," she added with a wink. "Have you ever seen a vaudeville show?" Olive sat up straighter and nodded. "So what would you say vaudeville is, exactly?"

Olive frowned. "The one I saw had dancers, and a comedian, an acrobat . . . oh, a magic act . . ."

"Exactly," Maude said. "A vaudeville show is a collection of different acts, which is what makes it so exciting. Rather than casting new members into the same old roles over and over, my show changes depending on the talent I find. Much more effective that way, as it allows everyone to play to their strengths. Before Tanisha, for example, I never had a juggler in my show. But once I saw what she could do, well . . . I simply had no choice but to create an act around her marvelous skills."

Olive shivered in anticipation. "What's the show called?" she asked eagerly, and Maude closed her eyes. When she spoke, her voice was full of reverence.

"*Eidola.*"

"*Eidola,*" Olive echoed. "What does that mean?"

Maude studied her for a long moment. "Eidola is . . . a place," she said at last. "A fantasy world I invented during my miserable childhood. Eidola was my escape, where I went in my mind when the real world was too unbearable. And everyone you just met, my wonderful cast—they are a part of this show not just because of their extraordinary talents but because they all know what it feels like to be alone, or outcast, or unloved. That is the one thing about this show that never changes, no matter what the acts are. *Eidola* is about *escape,* about being a part of something better. Something amazing." She paused, her eyes searching Olive's face. "That's what brought you here yesterday, isn't it? You needed an escape as well."

"Yes," Olive whispered.

"And why is that?" Maude asked gently. "What is it you're running away from?"

Olive hesitated before answering.

"My mother . . ." She paused, and Maude waited silently.

"She's always pushed me to do my best at everything because she wants me to be as successful as she was. But after last summer, when my dad . . . when he died, it got worse. No," Olive corrected herself. "Not worse. It *changed*. Before, when she'd lecture me for messing up an audition or singing off-key, it felt like she just wanted me to do well because she cared about me. But now she just expects me to fail. It's almost like she *wants* me to. Sometimes I . . ."

She tried to press her lips together. But the words came out anyway.

"Sometimes I think she hates me. And sometimes I— I hate her too."

It was an awful, awful thing to say. But maybe it was true.

Maude's eyes were closed as if she were absorbing Olive's words; the ones she'd said, but also the ones she hadn't said, because they were buried too deep and Olive did not wish to unearth them. Even though Olive was no longer speaking, Maude continued to nod slowly. And when she opened her eyes, Olive had the distinct impression Maude somehow knew more than what Olive had confessed out loud.

"We can all relate to *Eidola*," Maude said. "That's what makes this show so wonderful—it's more than just a show. It's an escape, a *home*, for all of us. Including you."

Olive's throat was too tight to respond, so she merely nodded. Smiling, Maude stood and gestured to the piano.

"Let's begin."

9

Destined for the Spotlight

The sun was just beginning to set behind the city's towering skyline when Olive finally left Maudeville. Her throat felt raw and open, and her head had that fuzzy, just-woke-up sensation. The boy in the alley poked his head up from behind the dumpster and watched her go, his expression dark. Olive barely noticed him. She practically floated down the street, still humming under her breath.

She couldn't remember ever being this happy. The songs in *Eidola* seemed to be written just for her; every word, every note, resonated deep inside her like plucking strings. And lessons with Maude were far more effective than with her mother. Laurel encouraged Olive to sing like Laurel. Maude encouraged Olive to sing like Olive, a better Olive. It was almost as if Maude could draw beautiful music from her—a physical feeling, like a thread tugging in her lungs.

Humming turned to flat-out singing as Olive left the theater district. A few pedestrians smiled as she passed, and a popcorn vendor rolled his eyes, but Olive didn't care. Her voice grew even louder when she saw the library up ahead. She sang until she saw her building, and then the song died in her throat.

The doorman would still be on the lookout for her. If he saw Olive come in, he'd tell her mother. And Mrs. Preiss would know exactly how Olive had snuck out. She'd never make it back to Maudeville again.

Her only choice was to go back the way she had come— the fire escape. But the ladder dangled several inches above Olive's fingers, too high to reach even when she jumped.

Olive turned in a slow circle, examining the alley. Trash cans lined the walls, overflowing with stuffed garbage bags. And there, on the corner facing the street, was a chair.

The coffee shop, Olive realized. She edged her way closer, keeping to the wall. The Marinos always added a few tables and chairs outside during the summer months. Mr. Preiss used to joke that having a coffee shop next door was the sole reason they had bought this particular penthouse. And the Marinos joked in turn that they only stayed in business because of Mr. Preiss. The café had been struggling lately, although Mr. Preiss's death wasn't to blame for that. Most businesses were desperate for customers these days.

Still, the Marinos were very nice, and Mrs. Marino gave Olive a free muffin every time she dropped by. Olive was sure they wouldn't mind her borrowing a chair.

Glancing up and down the street, Olive grabbed the chair and hurried back to the fire escape. She set the chair beneath the hanging ladder and stepped up. By standing on her tiptoes and stretching as high as she could, she just managed to grip the bottom rung.

It took Olive nearly a full minute to pull herself up enough to grab the second rung, then the third. She hooked her leg around the ladder and paused to catch her breath.

With one last glance at the coffee shop chair beneath her, Olive began to climb. She climbed from one balcony to the next, moving so quietly that not even Tinkerbell the shih tzu heard her on the sixth floor. At last she made it to the landing outside her father's study. She'd already swung one leg over the windowsill before noticing the door.

It was open.

Olive froze, half inside, half out. She'd shut that door behind her, she was certain. Hardly daring to breathe, Olive listened carefully. The penthouse was silent. After several long seconds, Olive pulled herself the rest of the way inside and slowly, slowly closed the window, accidentally nudging the telescope with her elbow. She crept across the room, her heart constricting painfully when she saw her father's desk. All the items were still there—map, papers, pens. But now they were organized, tidy.

Mrs. Preiss had been in the study.

Heart pounding in her ears, Olive left the room and closed the door behind her. She glanced at her bedroom door—also closed, just as she'd left it. Smoothing her windblown hair with her fingers, Olive squared her shoulders and marched down the hall. She would simply pretend that she'd been in her room this whole time and hope against hope her mother hadn't bothered to check.

Crossing the living room, Olive peered into the kitchen. Her mother sat at the table, head bowed over the mail. She didn't look up when Olive stepped inside.

"You can make a sandwich for dinner," Mrs. Preiss said shortly. "I bought groceries today."

"Okay." Olive hurried over to the pantry and examined its contents: a bag of lentils, a box of oatmeal, a jar of peanut butter, a loaf of bread. Her stomach rumbled with displeasure. It felt like ages since Olive had last had a truly good meal. Pot roast with buttery red potatoes, crispy fried artichokes with lemon, meatballs in spicy tomato sauce . . .

As if she could hear Olive's thoughts—or perhaps her stomach—Mrs. Preiss scowled. "This electricity bill is even higher than last month's. If I can't convince the arts center to refund that check for theater camp, I'm not sure what we're going to do."

The jar of peanut butter slipped from Olive's hand. She caught it just before it hit the tiled floor, her face burning. Guilt writhed around her insides like a snake. Maybe her mother was a bit overbearing, but she'd scrimped and saved for Olive to attend that camp in the hope that it would finally lead to a career for her daughter—not to mention an end to their financial woes. And Olive had just run away. She might as well have thrown the last of their cash into the fireplace.

Although . . .

Anger slowly began to eat up Olive's guilt. Maybe she'd run away from camp, but that had been her mother's fault. Parents weren't supposed to watch the auditions, and Olive would have done well if Mrs. Preiss had just let her sing her own song. Besides, now Olive had been cast in a show—a *real* show, a professional one, just like Mrs. Preiss wanted. Proof that Olive *was* destined for the spotlight after all.

For the briefest of seconds, Olive considered telling her mother all about Maudeville. Then, just as quickly, she decided not to. Mrs. Preiss was so short-tempered these days—and had so little faith in her daughter—that she was likely to snap at Olive for making things up. No way would she believe that Olive had successfully auditioned for anything. And if she knew Olive had snuck out, she'd probably lock her in her room for the rest of the summer.

Not worth the risk. *Eidola* would be Olive's secret until opening night. In the meantime, Mrs. Preiss could just keep selling their belongings, emptying their home. It didn't matter. Olive had Maudeville now.

Olive pulled a knife out of the drawer, unscrewed the lid of the peanut butter jar, and began making her dull supper. Under her breath she hummed the songs Maude had taught her, and she tried to imagine what the other acts would be like—the magic, the juggling, the fire-eating.

She was so distracted by these happy thoughts that she forgot to wonder why Mrs. Preiss had been in her husband's study for the first time in nearly a year.

10
A Very Nice Ghost

The rest of the week passed in an exhilarating blur. Olive and her mother were like opposing magnets, circling around some invisible force that kept them from direct contact. After breakfast each morning, Olive would sit in the living room, pretending to read a book, until Mrs. Preiss left for the day. Then she'd crawl down the fire escape and hurry to the theater for lessons with Maude. She returned home before the sun set, borrowing the coffee shop chair and climbing back up to her father's study. She would create some pretense—taking out the trash, checking the mail—to get past the doorman and slip into the alley, then move the chair back to the coffee shop before Mrs. Marino noticed it was missing.

Mrs. Preiss stayed out later each evening. Where she was and what she was doing, Olive wasn't sure. Selling more of their belongings, she figured. She didn't much care either way.

Eidola was all Olive could think about. Maude had a way

of coaxing the most beautiful music from Olive—already, she was singing far better than she ever had after countless vocal exercises with her mother. Memorizing music had never been this easy—by Friday, Olive knew the lyrics backward and forward. But it wasn't just that. She *understood* these songs, the purpose of every word, every note. It was as if they had been written for her specifically, and she'd been waiting her whole life to find them.

Olive saw the other cast members only in passing during breaks; she was too busy learning her part to watch them practice their acts. Tanisha often wandered the corridors, shoulders hunched, nose buried in a book Olive vaguely recognized from her father's collection, though Tanisha's copy looked much newer. She would smile and wave timidly at Olive but never said more than a few words. Mickey, in contrast, had a presence that could likely be felt on the moon. When he laughed, no matter where he was, the jovial sound seemed to rattle the whole theater. Valentine and Eli were usually in the kitchen when Olive went for a glass of water. Each time, Olive would almost ask Val where her (or his? Olive still couldn't quite tell) assistant was during breaks. But she stopped herself every time. Juliana seemed nice, but Olive didn't need friends—not when she had a show to focus on.

She liked all the cast members very much, though, and she couldn't wait to see their acts. Tuesday, Maude had promised, they would all begin rehearsing together. Olive knew that thought would be the only thing that would get her through the next three days without Maudeville.

She sang softly to herself as she crossed the lobby on Friday afternoon. But when she heard a muffled sob, Olive froze. She crept quietly across the marble floor, drawing nearer to the sound of the crying girl. The eyes of the portrait-Maudes watched her closely.

". . . he thinks I should leave, but I can't, because of you . . ."

Olive peeked around the column closest to the door and gasped.

"Oh!" Juliana spun around, wide-eyed, her face streaked with tears. Next to her, the air shimmered, and before Olive could decide whether she'd really seen the thing she thought she'd seen, it had vanished.

For a moment, the two girls simply gaped at each other. "Are you okay?" Olive asked at last. Her eyes strayed to the spot where the air had briefly seemed like more than air. Juliana stepped in front of it in a protective sort of way.

"I'm fine, it's nothing."

"Was that . . ." Olive hesitated. Her every nerve ending tingled, static covering her like a second layer of skin. "Was that a ghost?"

Juliana wiped her cheeks on her sleeve. "Yeah. There're lots of them around here." She caught the frightened look on Olive's face and gave her a feeble smile. "Don't worry. He's a very nice ghost."

"Who is he?"

"Um . . ." Juliana swallowed visibly. "Knuckles. He's in the orchestra." Her red eyes darted nervously around the lobby before focusing on Olive again. "You'll meet him soon, right? Maude said we'll all be rehearsing together next week, onstage. Everyone's so excited to hear you sing."

Olive tried not to look too pleased or too nervous. "I can't wait to see the rest of the show," she said. "Especially you and Valentine—I love magic acts. Does she really saw you in half? Oh, I mean, he! Or . . ." Olive trailed off, face suddenly aflame. But Juliana didn't seem to notice her embarrassment.

"Yup, I get sawed right down the middle," she replied. "And Val's not a he or a she."

Olive blinked. "Oh. So . . . what should I say?"

"They."

"They?" Olive repeated. "How do you know?"

"I asked them." Juliana toyed with her ponytail. "Anyway, I should get back to rehearsal. It was nice to see you again."

"Nice to see you too," Olive echoed. She watched as Juliana hurried to the double doors, giving Olive a quick wave before slipping inside the auditorium. Confused and deflated, Olive left the theater. Juliana had clearly been unwilling to tell Olive the truth, but what was she hiding? The way she'd stepped in front of the spot where the ghost had been, then hastily reassured Olive that all the theater's ghosts were friendly . . . maybe she'd lied so as not to scare Olive off.

Olive was so preoccupied she didn't hear the boy from the alley approaching. When he touched her shoulder, she screamed.

"Jeez, sorry!" He backed away, palms flat.

Olive scowled at him. "What do you want?"

The boy glanced over his shoulder at the theater. "Are you leaving?"

"Obviously."

"For good?"

Upon closer inspection, Olive noticed that the boy's eyes were pinkish, and his voice sounded hoarse, as if he'd been yelling or crying. His clothes—the same ones from earlier this week—were even dirtier now, and his fingernails were caked with grime. She remembered when she'd first seen him, rummaging around in the dumpster, and she realized with a pang that he might not have a home to return to.

"No, I'll be back Tuesday," she said, shifting to a kinder tone. "Um . . . what's your name?"

"Felix Morella."

"Oh." Olive attempted a smile. "I'm Olive Preiss."

"I know."

Olive opened her mouth to ask how, then decided he was probably lying. "Well," she said. "Nice to meet you."

"Wait!" Felix moved forward when she turned to leave. "Just wait a sec."

Olive eyed him warily. "What?"

"Look." Felix stood at her side and gestured at Maudeville. "Really *look* at it. What does it look like?"

Frowning, Olive looked. The grand, curved steps were flanked by two large columns, the granite flecked with sparkling silver. The colorful mosaic surrounding the entrance practically glowed, and the lights around the marquee were just beginning to twinkle as the sun dipped behind the theater. Olive pictured *Eidola! Starring Olive Preiss* on that marquee in bold black letters. For a moment, she actually saw it and smiled to herself.

"It's beautiful."

Felix made a frustrated noise, and Olive flushed a little. She hadn't meant to say that out loud.

"I have to go," she said quickly. "It's getting late."

"Don't come back."

"Excuse me?"

His voice was low and urgent. "Don't come back here. It's dangerous."

A weird, dry laugh escaped Olive. "Dangerous? How?"

"Because you can't *see* it!" Felix cried, riffling his hands through his hair in frustration. "Listen, it's not too late, you can—"

Olive stepped back, alarmed. "Stop," she whispered. "Please stop."

Felix fell silent. Olive glanced from him to the dumpster. "I'm sorry," she said shakily. "I really am. I'm sorry . . .

I have to go." His shoulders slumped, but he did not protest when she turned away and hurried down the empty street.

It's dangerous. Olive shook off these words. The boy was troubled, obviously. He ate food out of the dumpster; he didn't even have a change of clothes. And he was afraid of the theater, which was ridiculous . . . or was it? Olive frowned. Juliana had said Knuckles was nice, but he'd left her in tears. And Felix was too scared to even go inside.

Perhaps the ghosts of Maudeville weren't as kind as everyone claimed.

11
Out of Mind

The weekend was too hot and too long. Mrs. Preiss had placed electric fans in front of the open windows, circulating the humid air from outside throughout the penthouse. Olive spent Saturday and Sunday in her room. She desperately wanted to practice, but she couldn't let her mother hear. And with every hour that passed, the songs from *Eidola* slipped further from her mind.

By Sunday night, Olive was genuinely alarmed. It had been only two days, but somehow her memories of Maudeville were as faint as if she'd last visited years ago. The lyrics were vanishing, the melodies wavering and off-key. Panicking, Olive closed herself in her stuffy closet and tried to sing her favorite song, a haunting ballad that came just before the magic act. *"Bottomless floods and boundless vales, and . . ."* Olive squeezed her eyes closed. "No, that's not it. *Bottomless vales and boundless floods, and caves . . .* no, *chasms . . .* oh, come *on!*"

Frustrated, she flung her music folder at the closet door

and covered her face with her hands. In the dark behind her eyelids, she pictured herself onstage. Every seat was filled, all eyes on her as the spotlight hit. . . .

A different kind of warmth spread through her. Not the unpleasant, sticky late-summer mugginess. A comforting heat that started deep in her lungs and crept up her throat. Lowering her hands, Olive started the song again.

She remembered every word.

That night, Olive dreamed about *Eidola*. During breakfast, she saw the stage every time she blinked. Mrs. Preiss was irritated by her daughter's distracted behavior and, before going out, assigned her several chores to do throughout the day. The only bright side was that Olive had the penthouse to herself. She sang while she scrubbed the floors and dusted the furniture. After dinner, she fell onto her bed, still reeking of detergent, and slept deeply.

On Tuesday morning, Olive could barely eat her oatmeal. The oppressive heat and lingering smell of bleach made the penthouse unbearable. At last, Mrs. Preiss wrote a new list of chores and left for the day. Olive watched out the window until she saw her mother hurrying down the street to catch the bus. Once again, Olive briefly wondered where Mrs. Preiss was going. But the second her mother was out of sight, she was also out of mind.

Olive raced to her father's study, threw open the window, and climbed down the fire escape at top speed. She let go a rung too soon, and her feet smacked the pavement, sending a shock wave up through her knees.

"Olive?"

Spinning around, Olive stared at Mrs. Marino, who stood at the corner wiping off one of the coffee shop's patio tables. Brushing a lock of limp, graying hair off her forehead, the woman squinted at Olive through tiny spectacles. "Are you okay, hon?" Her eyes flickered to the ladder hanging over Olive's head.

"Fine!" Olive said, a little too brightly. "Just, um . . . taking out the trash." She gestured vaguely to one of the garbage cans, which she realized a second too late was empty. But if Mrs. Marino suspected anything, she didn't show it.

"Haven't seen you in a while!" she said cheerfully, tucking the rag into her apron pocket. "How've you been?"

"Great!" Olive chirped. "Really great."

"Good, good." Mrs. Marino tilted her head in a sympathetic sort of way. "And your mother?"

"She's fine."

"Glad to hear it. I'm about to take a batch of lemon bars out of the oven." Pulling the door open, Mrs. Marino smiled at Olive. "How about one or two on the house?"

"Thank you!" Olive said. "But I—I've got some errands to run for my mother. Maybe later?"

"All right, dear!" Olive thought she heard Mrs. Marino call something else, but she was already hurrying down

63

the street. She felt bad for being so rude, but after three days away from Maudeville, she could think of nothing but returning.

By the time she passed the Alcazar, Olive was panting and damp with sweat. A rustling noise from the alley caught her attention. Turning, Olive saw that the dumpster lid was up. She could just make out Felix's messy black hair as he rummaged around inside, tossing brown banana peels and tin cans over his shoulder. As if he felt her gaze, Felix looked up.

"You came back." He didn't sound surprised.

Olive shrugged. "Yeah."

They stared at each other for a moment. Then Felix held out a moldy orange. "Hungry?"

His lips twitched a little, and Olive found herself trying not to smile too. "You know, there's a fruit stand on the corner."

"I know."

"I, um . . ." Olive fished a few coins from her pocket and held them out awkwardly. "Here."

"What's that for?"

"For food," Olive said, flustered. "You shouldn't have to eat out of the dumpster."

A strange expression crossed his face. "You think that's gross, huh?"

By now, Olive was blushing furiously. "Look, will you just take this?"

"No, but thanks," Felix said. "That's really nice of you."

He spoke without a trace of sarcasm, and while he wasn't smiling, he didn't look offended either. Olive's face still felt as though it were on fire.

"You're welcome," she said uncomfortably. After a few seconds, she realized she was still holding out the coins and stuffed them hastily back in her pocket. "Well . . . see you later."

"See you."

Nodding, Olive turned and headed up the stairs. She'd half expected Felix to argue with her, tell her the theater was dangerous, once again try to stop her from going in. But he watched her go in silence. The double doors closed heavily behind her, the sound echoing in the empty lobby.

Olive paused to collect herself just outside of the auditorium, smoothing her hair and wiping the sweat off her brow. She could hear the buzz of voices inside, and a fresh wave of excitement flooded through her, now tinged with anxiety. Olive's eyes flickered from portrait to portrait. The Maudes all smiled, and her nerves quieted. She smiled back.

Lifting her chin, Olive pulled open the auditorium doors and was greeted by a floating severed hand.

12

The Only Thing Visible in the Darkness

The fingers wiggled as if to say hello. Frozen in shock, Olive barely had time to register the fact that the hand was transparent before it zoomed off toward the orchestra pit, where a jaunty polka seemed to be coming from the piano, despite the lack of a pianist. The hand disappeared behind the lid, and a moment later, a tinkling melody joined the chords.

Olive gazed at the scene in front of her in awe. A massive *thing* hung from the rafters in the back—oval, white, and completely wrapped in what appeared to be glistening white thread, like an enormous cocoon. Perhaps it was just Olive's imagination, but the thing glowed ever so slightly.

The stage seemed to have expanded since Olive had stood on it last Monday. It was as if the theater was bigger on the inside than its exterior implied. In fact, the stage was now so large that it accommodated the entire cast, all of whom were in the middle of their own private dress rehearsals.

Tanisha stood on the right, flinging dozens of snow

globes in a dizzying pattern in the air. She caught them all effortlessly, occasionally letting them roll down her shoulders or balancing one on her knee while juggling the rest. The globes flew higher and higher, each filled with its own raging snowstorm, and to Olive's eyes they seemed to hover overhead longer than the laws of physics would allow.

Mickey's fire-breathing act dominated the entire rear half of the stage. He paced back and forth, twirling his torch as the flames grew bigger and brighter. Stopping on the left side, he leaned back and, in one swift move, dipped the entire fiery torch into his mouth. Then he let out a magnificent billow of flames in a silent roar. The fire swirled around and around the giant white cocoon, and Olive, remembering Maude's story, had a brief, horrifying mental image of the entire theater burning to the ground. But Mickey stepped forward with his torch held out, looking every bit like a sorcerer with his staff. And somehow, incredibly, the flames *reversed,* twisting around back into the torch. Olive stared in disbelief at the cocoon, which appeared completely undamaged.

A body suddenly dropped from the rafters, and Olive screamed. Eli twisted in front of the cocoon, clinging to a long elastic rope that stretched across the stage, parallel to the surface. It bent beneath his weight to form a V, slowing Eli's fall until he hovered inches from the floor before the rope catapulted him upward and out of sight. Olive waited, clawing her face with her nails, but he did not reappear.

On the far left of the stage, Valentine slowly circled an innocuous-looking cabinet and then stepped inside, closing the doors firmly. Olive barely had time to blink before a voice whispered in her ear:

"Impressive, right?"

Gasping, Olive turned to find Valentine at her side, wearing a rather mischievous grin. "How . . ." Olive sputtered, staring from the magician to the wardrobe and back again.

Val's grin widened. "I'll take that as a yes." They pointed to center stage just as the piano polka ended with a flourish. "You haven't even seen our ventriloquist yet. Our newest act—well, besides you. You're going to love this."

Between Tanisha's flying snow globes, the seemingly out-of-control fire now raging once more from Mickey's mouth, and Eli's heart attack–inducing stunt, Olive had barely noticed the small girl seated in the middle of the stage. Her cropped hair was dyed a shocking shade of blue that would have made Mrs. Preiss purse her lips in disapproval. She wore a ruffled black skirt, bright pink shirt, and scuffed Mary Janes, along with tons of brightly colored, chunky necklaces and bracelets. A dummy sat on her knee, about the same size as the girl. He was blond, with cartoonish freckles on both cheeks and glassy brown eyes, and his suspenders and bow tie were the same shade of blue as the girl's hair.

Olive sank into a chair, vaguely aware of Val taking the seat next to her. "How old is she?"

"Nadia?" Val sounded amused. "Seven, I guess. Like Aidan."

"Aidan? Is that the dummy's name?" Olive asked, and Val smiled.

"Just watch."

So Olive watched. Nadia's voice was high and clear as she chatted with Aidan and set up jokes for him to deliver the punch lines. The dummy's voice was only slightly lower than hers, but Olive had to admit that Nadia's ventriloquism skills were astounding. Her mouth didn't open at all when Aidan spoke—she even took a sip of water and gargled while he sang "Goosey Goosey Gander," each word perfectly audible. But as impressive as Nadia was, especially considering her age, Olive couldn't help thinking her act wasn't quite as magical as the others.

That is, until Aidan leaped off her lap and took a bow while Nadia slumped over in her chair.

Olive cried out in shock. The little boy saw her gaping and waved cheerfully before gathering the girl up in his arms and heading offstage, staggering a little under her weight. Olive turned to Val, her mouth still opening and closing soundlessly.

The magician laughed. "Not bad, right?"

"I don't . . ." Olive shook her head. "I don't understand what just happened."

"You just saw the greatest ventriloquist act in the

world—that's what happened," Val replied. "Aidan's amazing. He had you going, right?"

"Aidan . . . is the ventriloquist?"

"Yep."

"So Nadia is the *dummy*?"

"That's right."

"But she looked so *real*!" Olive cried. "And Aidan looked so . . ." She flailed her arms, mimicking his jerky movements. "He was a puppet!"

Val was still snickering. But before either of them could say another word, a throaty voice came from behind them.

"What do you think, darling?"

At the sight of Maude's warm, wide smile, Olive thought her heart would explode with happiness. "It's *wonderful*!" she exclaimed. "All of it, everyone is just . . ." She trailed off, unable to express herself any more clearly. Maude looked pleased.

"So glad you approve," she said, skirts rustling as she continued down the aisle. "But I bet you'll appreciate it even more from up here!"

Olive gazed at Maude's retreating form. It wasn't until Val gave her a gentle push that she realized she was supposed to follow.

Time to sing.

Olive hurried down the aisle and onto the stage, tripping a little on the steps. This was nothing like the first time she'd climbed up on this stage, in an empty and silent hall. This was more exciting—and more terrifying. Olive was itching to show everyone, including herself, what she was capable of when her mother wasn't present. But what if she *wasn't* capable? The rest of the cast was so extraordinarily talented and so effortlessly confident. What if Olive's mother fright really *was* just stage fright? What if she simply wasn't meant to be in the spotlight at all?

Taking a deep breath, Olive noticed the mime in the first row. She was fairly certain he hadn't been there a few seconds ago.

"Astaire, if you will . . ." Maude beckoned for him to join them, and he hurried forward with an eager expression. He gave Olive a tiny smile, and she found herself smiling back.

"Your name's Astaire?" she asked softly. The mime did a few halfhearted tap steps and lifted his imaginary top hat, and Olive laughed. "Right, sorry. I should've figured it out." Mr. Preiss loved Fred Astaire's movies; they had been among the many films Olive and her father would watch together on lazy Sunday afternoons.

She edged closer to Astaire as Tanisha and Mickey left the stage to join Valentine in the seats, Mickey still swinging his torch about carelessly (although it was no longer burning). Giant boulder props slid toward center stage from both sides. Olive craned her neck to see who was moving them but saw no one.

"Shall we try the opening number?" Maude gave Olive

an encouraging smile. Her hands twitched, but she nodded bravely. When Maude leaned closer, she tensed, bracing herself for the criticism.

"Don't worry," Maude whispered. "I know you'll be amazing."

Olive glowed.

And then Maude was gliding down the steps and into the aisle, and the lights were dimming until Olive could no longer see the seats. Astaire placed a cool hand briefly on her shoulder before hurrying offstage to await his cue. Olive sank down cross-legged in front of the boulders and hugged her knees to her chest. Squinting at the piano, she saw a pair of floating severed hands hovering over the keys. One gave her a quick thumbs-up, and she nearly laughed, despite her nerves. The hall went pitch black and she waited, Maude's praise still ringing in her ears. Olive gazed up at the massive white cocoon hanging overhead, the only thing visible in the darkness. Calm settled into her bones, and she relaxed completely.

Then the spotlight hit and the world shifted.

13
Her Dreamland

In the spotlight world, nothing existed but a pit. It was a deep, dark pit, the kind of deep that's just short of bottomless, the kind of dark that's just a shade lighter than nothing at all. It would have been a silent pit too, if it weren't for the singing.

The melody was sad but sweet, echoing off the rocks and rising higher and higher into the perpetual gloom. It came from the child huddled at the bottom.

She hadn't always been in this pit. Once upon a time, she'd had a home with a father who wanted her to see the stars, and a mother who wanted her to become one. But now the girl was alone, and stars were just a distant memory. That was why her song was sad. The sweetness came from her escape—her dreamland. She built this place with notes and lyrics: the mountains that toppled and then rebuilt themselves even higher; the seas that surged yet never found a shore; the golden trees that stretched endlessly into the clouds; the frozen lake surrounded by white lilies that bloomed eternally. Only the girl could find this place. It lay outside the reach of a compass.

And yet she believed her dreamland had life—for how wonderful can a place be if there is no companionship to be found? Just as the girl asked this in her song, a companion appeared.

He hung upside down in front of her, clinging to an invisible rope like a spider on a thread. The girl laughed in delight as he landed nimbly on his feet and began to entertain her with pantomimes. He walked into a strong wind that the girl could not feel but that nonetheless blew the beret right off his head. He cast a fishing line into her imaginary ocean and wrestled with a whale. He threw a lasso around the moon and tugged it down as a gift. And then he tied the end of his invisible rope around the girl's waist.

She stood motionless as he began to climb the rope. When he vanished in the gloom, she cried out in fear, because she had been abandoned before and could not find her way out of this pit alone. The grief she'd worked so hard to push down rose up her throat and choked off her pleas for help. She patted her waist and groped the air desperately, but her fingers found nothing. Just when the girl was ready to collapse in defeat . . . her feet left the ground.

Gasping, she gazed down as the bottom of the pit fell farther and farther away. She sang to it until it disappeared, and then she sang up to whatever was coming next. And soon a pair of hands, so real and so warm, took hold of her arms and lifted her out. The girl's relief quickly gave way to astonishment as the mime set her down. Hot tears blurred her vision, and a once-dead ember flared to life, filling her heart with hope. The girl blinked frantically, gazing around in awe.

Impossibly, her dreamland was spread out before her, all fiery skies and frozen lakes, boundless mountains that never stopped crumbling and radiant trees that never stopped reaching. And overhead was a black sky filled with infinite stars that could show any picture, tell any story, that she wanted them to. The mime stood in silence while the girl sang her gratitude and relief at having reached this place at last.

Eidola was real.

14
Wrong

The next morning was insufferable. Olive could barely sit still throughout breakfast. She picked at her flavorless oatmeal, silently willing her mother to leave. But Mrs. Preiss seemed in no hurry, mindlessly stirring her coffee with one hand and turning the newspaper pages with the other.

Before the downturn, the Preiss family used to split the newspaper during breakfast. Mr. Preiss would whip up French toast with powdered sugar, or poached eggs and grits, while Mrs. Preiss divvied up the sections—editorials for Mr. Preiss, entertainment for Mrs. Preiss, and cartoons for Olive. Olive's mother hadn't offered her the funny pages in a long time, but it didn't matter. Olive didn't find them funny anymore.

Fidgeting, she glared at her mother's hand and listened to the sound of the spoon clanking against the inside of the mug.

Clank.

Her manicure was rubbing off, little flecks of polish missing.

Clink.

A shiny pink callus had begun on the side of her finger.

Clank.

Her wedding ring was gone.

Olive stopped fidgeting. She sat very, very still, staring at the imprint still circling her mother's ring finger. With a jolt, she remembered returning to the penthouse yesterday to find Mrs. Preiss in the living room talking with someone. Olive had peeked around the corner and seen a handsome young man in a worn and ill-fitting but impeccably clean suit. Another buyer, she'd realized when he handed Mrs. Preiss a wad of neatly folded bills. Then he'd patted his breast pocket and smiled and thanked Mrs. Preiss profusely before leaving. Olive had briefly wondered what he'd bought, but she hadn't dwelled on it. Now, however, she knew the truth.

Her mother had sold her wedding ring.

Setting the newspaper down, Mrs. Preiss stood and took her dishes to the sink. Olive gazed at the back of her head, her hair pulled into a neat, frizzless bun. That ring had never left her finger, and now it was gone, swapped for electricity and oatmeal.

"School starts in less than a month," Mrs. Preiss announced abruptly, patting a short stack of library books on the counter that Olive hadn't noticed. "I've had a look at your summer reading list. Start with *The Cabinetmaker's Apprentice* and be prepared for me to quiz you on Friday."

Swallowing, Olive nodded. She remained in her chair while her mother gathered up her keys and her purse. It wasn't until Olive heard the front door close that she shot to her feet, grabbed *The Cabinetmaker's Apprentice,* and sprinted out of the kitchen. She shoved the book into her satchel with her music folder and made a beeline for the fire escape.

The alley was empty, and Olive snuck past the coffee shop before breaking into a run. She had never been so desperate to get away from the penthouse. In the theater district, she dodged tourists and bicyclists, nearly crashing into a haggard-looking boy walking at least a dozen dogs. It took almost half a minute to untangle herself from the leashes, and when she arrived at Maudeville at last, she was in a state of great irritation and sweatiness. She was pleased to see Felix waiting for her on the steps, as she now had someone on whom to unleash her foul mood.

"You can stop wasting your time," she said shortly, heading up the stairs without pausing. "I'm going to keep coming here whether you like it or not."

"Yeah, I kinda figured." Felix jumped two steps, blocking Olive's path to the entrance. "So I need your help."

Olive opened her mouth to tell him off, then realized with an unpleasant lurch that his eyes were red and watery. "What is it?" she asked in the kindest tone she could manage.

Felix took a deep breath. "Tell Juliana to leave."

Goose bumps broke out on Olive's arms despite the heat. "What?"

"Just tell her to leave the theater. Please."

Olive's heart was pounding too fast. "Is she in trouble?" she whispered, thinking of Knuckles the ghost. "Wait—how do you know her?"

"She's my sister."

Olive stared at him. "Your sister," she repeated. She could now see the resemblance so clearly—she felt foolish for having missed it before. "Why don't you just talk to her yourself?"

"I've tried." Felix's voice broke a bit. "She won't listen to me, but maybe she'll listen to you. I can't . . ." Pausing, he ducked his head. "Just try, please. Tell her to leave."

"But why?" Olive asked insistently. "Can't you at least tell me why?"

"Because this place isn't what any of you think it is." Felix gave the theater a contemptuous glance over his shoulder. "But you can't see it."

"What does that even mean?" Olive cried in exasperation. "It's a theater—what else could it be?"

Felix grimaced. "I don't know. I'd tell you if I did. All I know is when you look at this place, you don't see the same thing I do."

He slipped past her, heading down the stairs and toward the alley. Olive studied the granite columns, the glittering mural, the bright marquee. "What do you see?" she called after Felix. He turned around, his eyes traveling over the entrance before coming to rest on Olive.

"I see a theater too. But it's horrible," he said quietly. "Ugly and horrible and just . . . wrong."

And with that, Felix disappeared into the alley, leaving Olive alone on the stairs. She walked slowly up the last few steps and entered the theater. The lobby was as magnificent as ever, with its white columns and shimmering chandeliers. Olive craned her neck to stare up at them as she headed toward the auditorium, remembering how she'd first thought they were covered in cobwebs instead of strands of crystals. She squinted, and they sparkled even more dazzlingly.

Olive pulled open the auditorium doors, vowing to put Felix out of her mind until she could talk to Juliana. Right now, *Eidola* was waiting for her.

15
A Decided Lack of Solidness

Rehearsal was a weird and wonderful blur. Every time the spotlight hit her, Olive was transported—the hall, the seats, the stage, all seemed to melt away. She had heard of actors "losing themselves" in their performances, and she marveled at how true that statement was. But she was, at times, dimly aware that this was only a performance. It was like being trapped in a shiny bubble and getting the occasional warped glimpse of reality through the sheen.

After practicing the opening number, they moved on to the next act. Olive's skin tingled with excitement. Maude had not explained the details of the acts besides Olive's songs. It was intentional, she'd told Olive after yesterday's rehearsal. Olive's reaction of surprise and wonder to the invisible rope had been genuine, and now she could use that in her performance.

The first few chords of the reprise began, and when Olive sang, the boulder prop on which she and Astaire stood began to slide backward. Olive watched as a silver ring about the size of a dinner plate rolled out onto the stage . . . and then another . . . and another. The first ring curved around, and the others followed like a line of ducklings after their mother. Soon a dozen rings were spinning in a perfect circle in front of the boulder.

Tanisha strode out onto the stage and through the circle. Olive stared in amazement. Gone was the shy smile, the slightly hunched shoulders. This girl had the confident posture of a ballerina.

There was a flash of silver as Tanisha caught one of the rings around her ankle. With another quick dip, she scooped up a second ring and twirled it around her wrist. The circle of rings closed in on her with each one she grabbed up, and soon she was tossing them in the air while spinning others around her wrists, ankles, and neck. The rings flew higher and higher, flashing under the bright lights. One hovered briefly at Olive's eye level, and she blinked—perhaps she was imagining it, but the ring seemed bigger. A few seconds later another ring sailed past, now the size of a tire.

Olive edged closer to Astaire as the rings swelled to the size of hula hoops, soaring up into the rafters before plummeting back down. Tanisha was a blur, spinning and ducking and catching and flinging the now-giant rings. At last, with a warrior-like cry, she flung one, two, three, all twelve in rapid succession, past the massive cocoon and high up into the rafters. For a second or two, Olive gaped at the darkness, wondering where they'd gone. Then there was a *whoosh,* and Olive screamed and ducked.

The giant silver rings fell one after the other around her and Astaire. Dumbfounded, Olive blinked a few times. The rings were *floating.* They hovered around the boulder, starting with the smallest at the top and moving down to the largest, creating a sort of staircase. Astaire held out his hand, and Olive took it tentatively. She touched her toe to the top ring and was amazed to find it perfectly sturdy. Together, she and Astaire descended the steps. The moment they reached the stage, there was a loud *crack.*

Astaire pulled Olive out of the way as the boulder split straight down the middle. The two halves slid apart to reveal Tanisha, standing calmly in the hollow center with a snow globe in each hand. She tossed them one after the other in the air, holding one hand behind her back while easily juggling with the other. After a few seconds, she switched hands, tossing a third globe into the mix. Back and forth went her hands, one juggling while the other pulled more globes seemingly out of thin air from behind her back, until dozens of globes flew overhead in an elaborate pattern.

In the orchestra pit, other sounds had begun creeping in to join the piano: an ominous low brass drone, a cello's mournful countermelody, the tinkling of wind chimes, the trill of a flute. They crescendoed, the chords becoming increasingly dissonant, the notes huddling closer together as if they were afraid. But Olive was so captivated by Tanisha's performance she didn't notice the gradual swell of sound until—

Gong!

Olive shrieked, gripping Astaire's cool hand when the auditorium momentarily went black. The mime squeezed back just as what looked like lightning flashed overhead. The stage lights returned, blue now instead of white. It took Olive a moment to register what she was seeing.

Tanisha spun, ducked, twisted, always catching each globe before it hit the ground. Only now . . . Olive squinted to be sure.

They were empty. Hollow glass globes soaring in a pattern that defied gravity.

No sooner had Olive wondered where the snow had gone than she felt something tickle her neck. She touched the spot, and her hand came away cold and wet. Another tiny something tickled her arm, then her cheek. Soon dozens, hundreds, *thousands* of snowflakes were falling across the stage, gently twirling in the wind created by Tanisha's ferocious juggling.

A minor arpeggio reached Olive's ears—her cue—and she drew a deep breath. Then she glanced down into the orchestra pit and faltered. A pianist sat on the bench, fingers moving over the keys. An elderly man with a receding hairline and bib overalls—and a decided lack of solidness.

Olive gazed at the ghost, her mouth still hanging open. She'd only spotted glimpses and glimmers of ghosts before, but nothing like this . . . this *person,* this transparent-yet-very-real person, playing minor arpeggios as if it were a perfectly normal thing for a spirit of the deceased to do. He glanced up at Olive and smiled, lifting one hand to waggle his fingers in greeting. Olive stifled a cry—the hand had separated from his arm at the wrist. It scratched his head and brushed off his collar before rejoining its limb. Both hands fell heavily on a dark, dramatic chord . . . and stopped.

Astaire gently nudged Olive's elbow, and her face went hot. She'd missed her cue. Instinctively, Olive looked out into the crowd for her mother's sharp, disapproving gaze. Her knees started to wobble, and her stomach flipped over, and she felt with absolute certainty that the only thing left to do was to flee the stage before it was spattered with oatmeal.

But before she could take one shaky step, the pianist caught her eye and gave her an encouraging smile. His transparency flickered in an almost teasing way, as though daring her to really see him. His fingers began pressing the keys at a slower, more deliberate tempo, severed hands moving slightly out of sync with his arms.

Olive smiled back. Taking a deep breath, she sang.

The second number was more upbeat than the first, pushed along by a bouncy bass pulse and staccato sleigh bells. Though her voice trembled over the first few notes,

Olive quickly recovered. She spread her arms wide and tilted her head back, snowflakes dotting her cheeks and sticking to her eyelashes. With a wicked grin, Tanisha began to hurl the globes at Astaire. He dodged each one with that same controlled sort of flailing as his tap dancing. Olive's voice warbled again over the lyrics, but this time it was from trying to hold back laughter at Astaire's expression of exaggerated mock terror.

He ducked and floundered as the globes sailed past him— and then, impossibly, swung around and sped back toward Tanisha like boomerangs. She flung them with greater intensity, and soon Olive was digging her fingernails into her face, waiting for one of the glass globes to clobber Astaire's head or bash his nose in. But the mime evaded each and every one. At last, he spun around in a few rapid, impressive pirouettes, then collapsed on the stage, tongue lolling out. Tanisha heaved each globe up as it returned to her, and the invisible orchestra ended the number with one last *gong!*

Olive squinted up at the rafters. She thought she'd seen a flurry of movement where the globes had vanished in the dark. As the house lights rose, Astaire stood and dusted himself off, and Tanisha set down her globes. Olive noticed that neither of them looked the least bit winded, and she wiped the sweat from her brow self-consciously before turning to the orchestra pit.

"I see the piano player," she said slowly. "And I see the other instruments, so why can't I see those musicians?"

"They don't all show themselves," Tanisha explained. "I've never seen most of the ghosts here. Just the seamstresses. And Knuckles, obviously."

She waved to the pianist, and one of his severed hands waved back cheerfully. A chill passed over Olive despite the heat from the lights overhead. "Knuckles? *That's* Knuckles?"

"Yeah." Tanisha stretched her arms. "You should ask him about his hands sometime. It's a great story."

But Olive was barely listening. She watched as the kindly-looking ghost leafed through his music with one hand. A single sheet fell to the floor, and his other hand drifted down to retrieve it. Knuckles caught her eye and smiled, but this time Olive couldn't smile back.

This was the ghost who had made Juliana cry.

16

Make-Believe Games

Hours later, Olive thought she might collapse onstage right next to Astaire. Maude had insisted on going through the juggling act again and again, each time finding something new to improve upon—but with kind, encouraging words, not the harsh criticism Olive was used to. Tanisha's moves grew flashier, Astaire's reactions more flamboyant, and Olive's voice stronger. Confident, even.

It was a strange feeling. Strange, but not unpleasant.

Her ears were still buzzing when she left the auditorium, waving goodbye to Tanisha and Astaire. Halfway across the foyer, Olive suddenly remembered Felix's message for Juliana.

She doubled back, humming under her breath as she hurried up the stairs. Her plan was to look in the rehearsal room first, but just as she passed the bathrooms—

"Olive!"

Olive spun around to see Juliana's head poking out from the entrance to the kitchen. "I was just looking for you."

"Sorry I didn't watch your first rehearsal, but I was sick all morning," Juliana said, leading her to the pantry. She pulled open the doors, revealing mostly barren shelves, and sighed. "Slim pickings, as usual."

Olive nodded in understanding, watching as Juliana grabbed a box of crackers. It dawned on her that this was the first time she'd seen anyone at the theater eat.

Juliana headed to one of the tables and plopped down on the bench. She peered inside the box before offering it to Olive. "Mostly crumbs, but there're still some good ones in here. Want one?"

"Sure." Olive took a cracker but didn't eat it. "Um . . . I talked to Felix today."

Juliana froze, cracker halfway to her mouth. She lowered it slowly.

"I know he's your brother, and . . ." Olive took a deep breath. "He wants me to tell you to leave Maudeville because you're in danger. And I don't know what he's talking about, but if Knuckles is—is threatening you, I want to help. We can tell Maude, and she'll take care of it."

Juliana's expression had changed rapidly as Olive spoke, from hope to frustration to confusion. "Knuckles?"

"That's who you said you were talking to in the lobby the other day, right?" Olive asked. "When you were crying."

"Oh." Juliana squeezed her eyes closed. "Right. No, I wasn't crying because of Knuckles. I'd just had a fight with Felix and came back inside and saw . . ." She shook her head, and her voice took on a steely edge. "I can't leave. I don't *want* to leave. And Felix knows why. If he were a decent brother, he'd . . ." She trailed off again.

Olive shifted uncomfortably. "He says the theater is . . . is bad, or something," she said. "He says it looks *wrong*. What does he mean?"

Juliana toyed with her cracker. "I don't know. He's delusional," she said bitterly. "He's always hated this place, even though it was the best option we had when we ran away."

Olive stayed silent. So she'd been right—Felix didn't have a home. Nor did Juliana.

"You live here?" she asked, and Juliana glanced up.

"Yeah. All the rest of the cast does too." She smiled tentatively. "Maybe you could live here too, one day."

Olive looked away quickly, because that hopeful feeling had returned. "Maybe," she said. "But why would Felix rather live on the street than in here? Is he afraid of ghosts?"

Juliana was silent for a few seconds. "Sort of, yeah. He thinks he can get a job with some carnival, and he wants me to come. That's what we were fighting about the other day. I can't . . . I don't want to leave Maudeville. But he's so sure that there's something wrong with this place."

Olive watched her closely. Juliana blinked rapidly, turning the cracker over and over in her fingers.

"It's not like Felix to make stuff up," she continued slowly. "Even when we were little, he didn't like playing make-believe games, you know? But I needed them. I needed to pretend I was a princess, or a wizard, or . . . someone else. Some*where* else, any place that wasn't our house with our father." Her voice cracked slightly, and she shook her head. "But Felix didn't want to pretend. He wanted to get away for real. And . . ."

She stopped, staring at the cracker in her hand. Then she dropped it and stood abruptly.

"What?" Olive said, confused. "What's wrong?"

"N-nothing," Juliana stammered, clutching her stomach. "I guess I'm still just feeling sick. I should go lie down." She headed for the entrance, then glanced back at Olive. "Look, don't listen to anything Felix tells you, okay? He's just . . . his head's not right."

She left without giving Olive a chance to respond.

Sighing, Olive reached for the box of crackers and stopped. A fine coat of bluish-green dust covered the pads of her first finger and thumb. She glanced around, wondering where it had come from. After a moment, she shrugged and headed to the sink.

Olive pondered her conversation with Juliana as she scrubbed her hands clean. She wondered what could cause such a rift between a brother and sister, and why Felix hated the theater when everyone else loved it so. *His head's not right,* Juliana had said. And maybe that was true. But obviously, there was more to it than that, and Olive was determined to figure it out.

17
Some Nerve

Felix was not outside the theater the next day, a fact that disappointed Olive more than she cared to admit. And Juliana spent the afternoon in the rehearsal room with Valentine, working on their act. But there was someone else who might have the answers Olive was looking for, and she'd decided to talk to him the next chance she got.

In rehearsal, they moved on to Eli and his heart-stopping aerialist act. Olive nearly fainted the first time she saw the petite man flying from one silver hoop to the next—the very same hoops Tanisha had juggled. They floated through the air, gradually luring Eli out from the stage and over the orchestra pit, then the seats, until he was twisting and flipping around high overhead in that beautiful dome beneath the feathery winglike pattern.

Olive had dreamed about Tanisha's juggling act the night before, how the globes and hoops hung in the air in a way that would make a physicist weep, and she wondered again about the ghosts who made such magic possible.

There was Astaire's invisible rope too—surely it was ghosts lifting Olive out of her "pit" in the opening scene. And the beautiful white cocoon was always present in her dreams now. It would glow and tremble violently as something inside it struggled to break free. The real cocoon didn't shake, although a few times Olive thought she caught a tiny movement.

"It's the ghosts, right?" Olive asked Eli eagerly once he'd returned safely to the stage. "The ghosts are moving the hoops and all the other props?"

A small smile tugged at the corner of Eli's mouth. "Something like that" was all he said. But Olive knew she must be right, and whether the other ghosts were nice or mean, she hoped they would start to show themselves soon. Truth be told, Eli's act frightened her more than the other acts did. Watching him fly so high above the ground would be a lot less terrifying if Olive could see the ghosts who supported him.

But Knuckles remained the only ghost Olive could see. And he was also the person Olive needed to talk to. Juliana had said Knuckles hadn't threatened her, and Olive wanted to believe that was true. But she still approached the pianist with caution.

"Hello," she said tentatively. Knuckles glanced up from the sheet music he'd been studying and smiled. One of his hands hovered over the conductor's podium, waving a baton. The other swayed gently back and forth over the piano, palm up, as if relaxing in an invisible hammock. Olive forced herself not to laugh.

"Hi!" Knuckles's voice was bright and pleasant. "You sounded lovely today. One of the best singers we've had yet—and I've heard them all."

Olive blushed. "Thank you. How long have you been doing this show?"

"Oh, since the day I died," he said lightly. "Been dead almost as long as I'd been alive, and twice as happy."

"Really?" Olive said, taken aback. "What was wrong with being alive?"

Knuckles waved a handless arm dismissively. "Nothing *wrong* with it. In fact, I was pretty upset when I finally figured out I was dead. Then I realized I had it so much better." His wrinkled face softened as he gazed down at the piano. "All I wanted to do when I was younger was play. But I lost my hands in a factory accident when I was maybe a few years older than you. Learned to get by, but being a pianist wasn't so much of an option anymore."

All thoughts of Juliana and Felix momentarily disappeared, and Olive gaped at the ghost. "You lost your hands when you were a teenager?"

"That's right."

"And you found them when you . . . you . . ."

"Died?" Knuckles supplied, nodding. "Over fifty years later. Curled up on my usual park bench for the night, woke up, and walked away without realizing I was leaving my body right there in the park. My hands—well, the ghosts of my hands—found me. I thought I was hallucinating." He laughed, his eyes crinkling. "I chased them, and they led me to this very theater. Maude said they'd been playing piano here awhile. Developed minds of their own once they got away from me, apparently."

Olive did not know how to respond. Knuckles appeared unperturbed, even amused, but she felt terribly sorry for him. Then she remembered Juliana and stiffened her resolve. She opened her mouth to speak, but Knuckles beat her to it.

"I saw your audition, you know," he told her. "Marched right up on that stage and sang without waiting for an invitation. No wonder Maude loves you—you've got some nerve. She's never had much patience for the meek."

Olive lifted her chin, his words filling her with pride. Her mother had never said she had *nerve*. Quite the opposite, in fact. But Knuckles was right—here at Maudeville, Olive was perfectly confident onstage. It really had been mother fright holding her back all along.

Perhaps Olive was better off without her.

After a few seconds of silence, Knuckles's right hand waggled its fingers in her face. "Oh!" Startled, Olive waved it away. "Sorry, I was just . . . um . . . ."

"Distracted," Knuckles said with a cheerful grin, glancing up at the now-empty stage. "The others are probably at dinner—aren't you hungry? That's the only thing I miss about being alive," he added wistfully. "The food. Sometimes I think I'd give up one of my hands for some pork dumplings." His left hand made a rude gesture, which he ignored.

Olive smiled. "Oh—no, I don't live here. But I should get home." She paused, watching as his left hand twirled the conductor's baton between its fingers. "Knuckles?"

"Yes?"

She took a deep breath and looked into the ghost's kind eyes, trying to focus on him and not the tuba visible through his head. "I have a question about Juliana."

Knuckles nodded encouragingly. "What about her?"

"Did you . . ." Olive hesitated. "She seems upset about something, and I wondered if maybe you knew anything about it."

"Ah." Sadness flickered on his round, wrinkly face. "I do, in fact."

Olive tried not to sound too eager. "You do?"

"Of course," the ghost replied. "Juliana hasn't been the same since Finley." He said *Finley* as though it referred to an incident and not a person. "I keep trying to tell her it's for the best, but—"

"Liang, dear." The sound of Maude's husky voice caused Olive to jump. She spun around to find the woman right behind her, smiling at Knuckles. "Are you still talking Olive's ear off? I'm sure her mother won't appreciate her being late."

Startled, Olive looked at her watch. "Oh yes—I really should be going." She paused, glancing uncertainly at Knuckles. "Liang?"

"That's me," he replied good-naturedly. "You didn't think my mother named me Knuckles, did you?"

Olive laughed despite herself. "I guess not. I'll see you tomorrow."

"Till tomorrow!" Knuckles agreed, and his hands waved and somersaulted.

Maude gave Olive a warm smile. "Till tomorrow, darling."

Hurrying through the lobby, Olive went over her conversation with Knuckles. Whatever was wrong with Juliana, it had to do with Finley. The entire cast looked sad whenever the former star of *Eidola* was mentioned, which was understandable. But she couldn't imagine how Finley's death could have driven such a wedge between Juliana and her brother.

Olive checked the empty alley thoroughly before beginning her walk home. No Felix. And she'd dawdled too long—this was the latest she'd ever left the theater. She'd have to hurry to beat her mother home.

18
A Lion in the Stars

By the end of Friday's rehearsal, Olive's sides ached from laughing. They'd moved on to Aidan and Nadia's act, which was even more astounding up close—and, thanks to Astaire, even more hilarious. The mime was enamored with Nadia. He pulled a bouquet of posies out of thin air to present to her the moment she and Aidan appeared onstage. Olive, still squinting up at the dome and trying to see Eli in the suddenly dark auditorium, had not even noticed the boy and his puppet until she turned and found them standing beneath the giant cocoon.

She'd watched Aidan closely this time, now that she knew the secret of his act. But the young ventriloquist played the part of a dummy perfectly, slouching ever so slightly, his motions stilted and jerky, his mouth moving just out of sync with his words. Nadia, in contrast, was graceful and articulate. Her bright, offbeat look helped disguise some of her puppet-ness, from the electric-blue bangs nearly covering her glass eyes to the vivid pink paint on her wooden lips.

But Astaire was the most effective distraction. He hung on Nadia's every word, heaving great gasps at the most impressive tricks with her "puppet" and doubling over in silent laughter until tears rolled down his face after every punch line. And when the act ended with Aidan stepping forward and Nadia slumping over, as if her soul had left her body and entered his, Astaire swooned, falling back on the stage with his hand over his heart.

Olive thought about Aidan and Nadia all the way home, still marveling at their transformation. It was almost enough to distract her from the recollection that Eli had evaded her questions about Finley, as had Mickey. Both had looked distinctly uncomfortable when Olive mentioned the former star, and each had attempted to distract her in his own way: Eli by offering her a cranberry scone, Mickey by showing off an elaborate new move in his routine (and nearly setting Olive's hair on fire in the process).

And once again, Felix and Juliana were nowhere to be found. Tanisha had informed her that Juliana was rehearsing with Valentine again. But Olive had no explanation for Felix's absence. He couldn't have just given up—Juliana was his sister, and he felt she was in danger. Olive had the nagging sense that something bad had happened to him, and she pondered this as she climbed up the fire escape and slipped through the window.

The sight of her mother drove all these thoughts from Olive's mind.

Mrs. Preiss sat in Mr. Preiss's chair behind his desk, eyes cold and hard. Olive froze right next to the telescope. For a moment, she understood perfectly what it must feel like to be a ghost—the numbness of having someone you know stare straight through you.

"Mrs. Marino told me she's seen you in the alley." Mrs. Preiss's voice cut through Olive like steel. "She was worried you were developing an obsession with . . ."

Her eyes flickered to the window, and she didn't have to finish the sentence. Olive knew what she meant. Mr. Preiss's absence had its own presence, the invisible shape of him right in front of the open window. Olive had been standing in this exact spot next to the telescope the moment she'd first realized something was wrong. She'd been searching for a lion in the stars and had tugged her father's sleeve when she found one. He hadn't responded right away, and when Olive looked up, he was staring at the sky with an expression so lost, so empty, it sent a chill up her spine. He'd snapped out of it, but his "moods," as Mrs. Preiss called them, started to come more frequently and stay longer and longer. It was as if something evil had snaked in through the open window and stolen his soul, leaving behind an impostor father who did not love any of the things—or people—Olive's father had loved.

"Where," Mrs. Preiss said sharply. "Tell me where you've been."

Olive's spine stiffened. This was it—not the ideal circumstances, certainly, but the time had come for her to tell her mother the truth. And maybe there was a chance, however small, that she would finally be proud.

"I'm in a show."

Her mother's expression didn't even flicker. "A show."

"Yes." Olive's voice quaked a bit. "It's called *Eidola,* and . . . I have the lead role." When Mrs. Preiss didn't respond, Olive continued. "It happened after I ran away from theater camp. It started raining and I went inside this theater, and the owner heard me singing and she . . . um, she asked me to be in her show."

Tick. Tick. Tick. The clock hanging on the wall sounded louder in the silence after Olive finished. She swallowed and found that her mouth was dry. "It's a really good show," she added lamely. Her mother closed her eyes and exhaled sharply through her nostrils. For a moment, she looked and sounded so dragonlike that Olive half expected to see sparks.

"Try again," Mrs. Preiss said through gritted teeth. "And this time, the truth."

"It is the truth!" Olive exclaimed. "It's Maude Devore's theater. She used to be—"

"*Olive,*" her mother snapped. "Stop."

Olive closed her mouth and clenched her fists. Mrs. Preiss stood slowly.

"Until you decide to tell me where you've been going, you're not to leave this house. No checking the mail," she said, louder now over Olive's cry of protest. "No taking out the garbage, no visiting the coffee shop. I'm going to ask Mrs. Marino to look in on you while I'm gone during the day."

Hot tears prickled Olive's eyes. "But I'm in a show," she whispered. "I know I should've told you, but—can't you at least check the theater? It's right by the Alcazar. Talk to Maude—she'll tell you. . . ." Her mother shook her head, and Olive swallowed hard. "Why don't you believe me?"

"Because I've done my best to get you into countless school plays," her mother snapped. "Musicals at the community center, acting lessons, that talent show at the synagogue last spring, summer theater camp. And it's the same story every single time, Olive. You say you want to perform, I do everything I can to help you, and then when the time comes, you panic."

"But I didn't this time!" Olive cried. "I didn't panic, I didn't run away, and I didn't mess up—I did well. And it's because *you* weren't there!"

She stopped, breathing hard. Her mother's face contorted, but not with anger, as Olive had expected. In fact, this expression was so foreign to her features that it took Olive a moment to comprehend the emotion.

Pity.

"Stop living in a fantasy world, Olive," Mrs. Preiss said

at last. "We both know you couldn't possibly be in a show. You're simply not capable."

Olive's tears spilled over, and she made her way blindly out of her father's study. She stumbled down the hall and into her bedroom, slamming her door so hard it would have shaken the pictures right off her walls if there were any left to shake.

19

This Temporary Coffin

The curtains were drawn in Olive's bedroom all weekend, cocooning her in the dark. She ventured out only for meals, forcing down watery soup or lumpy oatmeal while avoiding eye contact with her mother, then returning to her bed. Nighttime was the worst because Olive couldn't sleep. She dreamed with her eyes open instead, watching glass globes and aerialists soar across her ceiling through rings of fire, dancing with puppets come to life. And every so often, she thought her door cracked open, just a bit, to reveal a pair of eyes glinting at her from the blackness of the hall. But when she turned on her lamp, her door was always closed.

Olive plotted her escape.

She plotted, but she didn't act. Because her mother watched her like a hawk. And also because the longer Olive was away from the theater, the more she lost her nerve. At Maudeville, Olive was the kind of girl who dared to chase her dreams. But trapped at home, her mother fright had returned, and she was meek once again.

Until Monday morning, when Olive found courage through fury.

The movers arrived before breakfast, thumping and bumping down the hall. Olive, who had been awake-dreaming about the juggling act again, briefly thought it was the sound of glass globes plopping onto the carpet. She blinked several times, imagining tiny grains of glass scratching behind her heavy lids. Then she shuffled to her door and peered out to see a short, thick-armed man back out of her father's study carrying one end of his desk, the telescope case balanced on top.

"What are you doing?" Olive croaked, but he didn't hear. The other end of the desk appeared, supported by another burly man. Next came a dolly stacked with boxes labeled *BOOKS,* then the empty bookshelf. The leather chair followed, along with the now-uncovered mirror, a sheet draped over the mover's shoulder. Olive caught a glimpse of her own horrified reflection and retreated into her room.

Her mother was selling her father's belongings.

His messy study, all that wonderful clutter, the maps and books and *History Haunts Us* coffee mug and shiny silver telescope. Gone. Now there would be no trace of Olive's father in the penthouse, no reminder of his existence, no reason for Olive to search the stars for stories.

The hole Olive had stitched up in her chest began to itch and burn. Panic seized her, and soon she was flying about her room, pulling clothes from her closet and socks and underwear from her dresser, shoving them unceremoniously into her satchel. She slipped out of her room and crept slowly down the hall, sticking close to the wall. Olive heard Mrs. Preiss's voice in the kitchen, and a rush of hot anger swept over her from head to toe.

The desk sat near the front door, boxes of books piled on top. Olive thought of the doorman downstairs, of the movers coming up and going down in the elevator. And without giving herself a chance to second-guess her plan, she opened the door on the right side of the desk and tucked herself inside.

It was a small space; Olive had to hug her knees with her satchel between her legs and her chest just to fit, and she couldn't quite get the door to close without a knob on the inside. She held her breath as footsteps approached.

A mover kicked the door closed, and Olive's hiding spot went black. She took shallow, shaky breaths, her head filled with the scent of wood and paper and, very faintly, her father's cologne. Then the desk lurched, and she pressed herself against the back so she wouldn't tumble out.

"Thing's heavier than it looks," she heard one of the movers mutter. The other just grunted in response.

And then they were bumping and thumping out of the penthouse. Olive did her best to track where they were; the movers set the desk down in the elevator, and she waited several minutes as they loaded the space with more of her father's belongings. She felt the elevator descend, and it was several more long minutes during which they unloaded it, saving the desk for last. By the time Olive heard the beeps and honks of traffic, her left leg had a cramp and her backside ached. She chanced a peek outside, pushing the desk door open just a crack, and was surprised to find herself not on the street but in the mover's truck.

Olive tensed, ready to scurry down the ramp before the movers noticed. But one appeared quite suddenly—he would have seen her for sure had it not been for the stack of boxes in his arms. With a gasp, Olive retreated and pulled her door as closed as possible. A moment later, there was a heavy scraping noise, and the door clicked shut.

Silence. The sounds of traffic were gone, somehow. No, Olive thought, straining to hear over her hammering heart. She could still hear the rush of cars, but it was muffled now. It wasn't until Olive pushed on the door and found that it wouldn't budge that she realized what had happened. The mover had pushed the stack of boxes right up against her father's desk.

She was trapped.

Suddenly choking for air, Olive leaned against the door with all her might. She kicked and shoved and clawed at the wood that was pressing her in, and a scream for help bubbled up in her throat, but she swallowed it back.

Because if she screamed, the movers would find her. And they'd bring her back up to the penthouse. Here was

Olive's choice: life with her mother, or this temporary coffin.

So she closed her mouth and closed her eyes and pictured a great open stage and a spotlight. Soon Olive was only distantly aware of the thuds as the movers finished loading the truck. She barely stirred when the truck roared to life and pulled away from the curb. She hummed to herself as it drove through the city streets, her shoulders banging into the walls of her small tomb every time the truck made a sharp turn. Olive didn't notice when the engine died and the truck sat still. Nor did she hear the muffled *slam! slam!* as the two movers exited. Hours passed with Olive curled up in a cramped little ball, and she didn't notice at all.

20
A Poisonous Seed

A great screeching noise jarred Olive quite abruptly from her dream. She gasped and instinctively pushed at the walls before fully remembering her situation. Then she fell quiet, listening to the sound of things being unloaded around her. The desk lurched, and she squeezed her arms around her now-numb legs to keep her balance as it was carried down the ramp and set heavily on the ground. When the footsteps faded, Olive pushed the door open.

Reddish-orange light assaulted her corneas. Through the tears blurring her vision, Olive saw she was facing a small pawnshop. Her father's leather chair and several boxes sat next to the entrance. Olive crept out of the desk, satchel over her shoulder, and nearly cried out at the sudden pins and needles she felt as the blood rushed through her legs. Gravel scraped her knees and palms as she crawled as fast as she could toward a nearby mailbox. It dawned on her that she'd forgotten to change out of her nightgown and slippers, and a mad giggle escaped her throat.

Safely hidden from the movers' view, Olive assessed her surroundings. Next to the pawnshop was a bookstore, cozy and welcoming, with a twisty staircase leading up to a loft visible through the glass door. On the corner, a couple sat at a tiny table beneath an awning that read *Doc's Oyster House.* Lifting a glass of wine to her lips, the woman glanced around. Her gaze fell on Olive, and her eyes widened in shock.

Bemused, Olive stared down at herself. Her knees were bleeding, her legs still quaked, and her nightgown must have caught on the desk, because there was a large rip in the bell sleeve. Tears and sweat coated her face, and she didn't need a mirror to know that her hair was a tangled, frizzy mess.

The woman gestured at Olive, and the man turned to look. When he flagged a waiter, Olive realized she had to go.

She pulled herself to her feet, willing her legs to function and wincing as the pins and needles tripled. Someone—the waiter, she thought—called after her as she took off in the opposite direction.

Olive crept down one block after another, trying and failing to avoid the stares of strangers. Any minute, a policeman would spot her and take her home. She had to find Maudeville . . . but she had no idea where she was. The sky was that bright burst of red the sun bleeds before dying, and Olive's panic increased with every passing second. Soon she would be alone in this monstrous kraken of a city at night.

Finally, she rounded a corner and spotted a familiar, stately building. The library! Her relief, however, was short-lived.

"Are you okay, sweetheart?"

Olive spun around to find a tall, thin woman looking down at her with kind eyes. Her lips pursed at the sight of Olive's skinned, dirty hands.

"Do you need help?" she asked, and then, without waiting for a response, said, "Ah, I see a few policemen right down there. Here, we'll just . . ."

But what they'd just do, Olive never heard. Because she was running toward the library as fast as her prickling legs would carry her.

She flew through the city like a ghost, wind whipping her nightgown around her bloody knees. She passed the library and increased her speed. Every time a car slowed down, her heart sped up. Every driver had her mother's piercing eyes.

But the monster was on her side tonight, its adrenaline spiked, blood pumping faster through its veins. Sirens wailed in the distance as Olive sprinted down block after block. Green lights flashed red to keep traffic out of her way as she tore across the wide streets. Vendors and shoppers and even police officers were so distracted with their own matters they barely noticed her.

Olive only slowed her pace once she'd reached the theater district. A few strangers still glanced at her with curiosity or disapproval, but the city's heart was always brimming with street performers and other odd types; a bedraggled child attracted much less attention here.

At the sight of Maudeville, Olive's heart soared. She dashed up the steps and pushed on the double doors.

They didn't budge.

Too out of breath to even cry out in frustration, Olive staggered backward and stared. Something small yet heavy sprouted in her stomach like a poisonous seed.

The theater looked . . . derelict. Letters hung askew on the marquee, and the glass covering the box office had a long, thick crack. Black scorch marks licked the mural, the tiny, jewel-like stones now a monotone gray. And the once-grand granite columns were chipped and crumbling, covered in layers of grime.

Setting her jaw, Olive marched up to the doors and pulled hard, hard, *hard*. Then she kicked the doors even harder and regretted it instantly. *"Ow!"*

"Well, that was pretty dumb. You're wearing slippers."

Olive whirled around. Felix leaned against the dumpster, and for some reason the sight of him tripled Olive's anger.

"Why's it closed up?" she demanded, gesturing at the stubborn doors. "Why's it all . . . different?"

"What's different?"

"Everything!" Olive yelled. "Maudeville! It's—it's ugly, it's old! What happened?"

"That's what it's always looked like," Felix replied, and the last lingering bit of Olive's patience vanished.

"It did *not*!" she screamed, and then she was pounding on the doors with her fists and yelling as loud as she could. When a deep, rusted *click* sounded, she froze in surprise. Slowly, slowly, the doors swung open.

The lobby was empty.

"Don't." Felix was at the bottom of the staircase now, his dark eyes wide with fear. "Don't go in there."

"What about Juliana?" Olive stepped inside and turned to face him. "Your sister's in here, and she's perfectly safe."

Felix shook his head vigorously. "She's *not* safe, she's—"

"So come find her!" Olive cried. "If you're so worried about Juliana, why don't you just come get her? Are you really so afraid of ghosts that you'd just abandon your own sister?"

Despite her anger, Olive regretted the words the moment they left her mouth. Because Felix didn't look mad, or confused, or afraid. He looked wounded.

"I *can't* go in. She throws me out whenever I try."

Swallowing, Olive took another step into the lobby. "Look," she told Felix shakily. "If you come with me, I'm sure—"

Before she could finish, the double doors between them swung closed with a *bang*. Olive jumped, her heartbeat mirroring the echo that bounced off the walls. Swallowing, she turned in a small circle.

"Hello?"

No answer. But the ghosts were here—they must be. It bothered Olive that she still couldn't see them all.

She crossed the lobby quickly, her slippered feet barely making a sound. The doors to the auditorium were locked, and when Olive pressed her ear to them, it was silent as a tomb within.

"Monday," she whispered. No rehearsal on Mondays, of course.

She padded over to the stairway, only to find those doors locked up just as tight. She knocked and knocked and called for Maude or Astaire, but no one came.

"They're probably in the kitchen," she assured herself, clutching her satchel closer. "They just can't hear me." Olive kept her eyes down as she spoke. Because the truth was, she could not bear to look around the lobby. It was too dark, too dingy. She did not want to see that the spider-silk-fine strands of crystals on the chandeliers now lacked any sparkle. She did not want to see the thick coating of dust that covered Maude's portraits so that the only things visible were eyes and teeth. This was Olive's home now, and it was beautiful. It had to be.

Forever and ever.

So Olive curled up on the floor in front of the auditorium, closed her eyes, and fell into a dreamless sleep.

21

A Thousand Spools of Thread

She awoke in an unfamiliar bed with a ghost sewing her sleeve.

Stiff and still as a corpse, Olive attempted to blink the sleep from her eyes. There were three ghosts in total—all women, and all dressed in heavy-looking old-fashioned dresses, with their hair pinned back in buns. Charcoal-lined eyes and crimson-stained lips stood out vividly on their otherwise pale, transparent faces. The one who was mending Olive's sleeve looked to be the youngest, her expression softer and more innocent than the others'. The one bandaging Olive's knees seemed nervous, eyes darting around anxiously. And the one who was overseeing their progress appeared to be the oldest, though not *old*. Worry lines creased the skin near her eyes, but she smiled encouragingly and placed a hand on the nervous ghost's shoulder. It passed straight through the girl, of course, but she relaxed a tiny bit nonetheless.

None of them spoke.

Olive watched them work in silence, not entirely convinced she was awake. She took in the details of her surroundings bit by bit: hard cot, a toilet and a sink, shelves lined with glass bottles giving off a vaguely astringent scent. An infirmary? But she wasn't ill. Although her right foot had a dull ache, and her hands and knees itched painfully. And her mouth was dry, and her throat burned, and her bladder was too full, and her stomach felt simultaneously swollen and hollow, as if a giant bubble of emptiness was expanding inside her.

"Eurgh."

The nervous ghost zoomed up to the ceiling and stared down at Olive, hands over her mouth. The other two, though momentarily startled by Olive's grunt, simply smiled. The oldest gestured to a tiny table next to Olive's cot. At the sight of the glass of water, the burn in Olive's throat intensified. She grasped it with trembling fingers and drank deeply, water sloshing down her front. The youngest ghost tied off the thread and clipped the extra length with a small pair of scissors. Olive admired her handiwork—she could hardly see where the rip on her sleeve had been.

"Thank you," Olive croaked. Though she had many questions to ask, the gnawing in her stomach and the ache in her bladder made it difficult to focus on anything else.

The oldest ghost floated back, motioning for Olive to sit up. Olive obeyed, wincing at pangs of pain in new places. It took nearly a full minute of effort for her to stand, with all three ghosts—the nervous one had rejoined the others with a sheepish expression—gathered around in support. Of course, that support turned out to be more moral than literal, as Olive discovered when her legs gave out and she fell right through the youngest ghost's open arms. Cheeks flushed with embarrassment, Olive pulled herself up off the floor and willed her limbs to function. She made her way to the toilet, and the three ghosts turned politely to give her privacy. After washing her hands and splashing cold water on her face, Olive followed the oldest ghost from the infirmary, legs quaking only a little bit, with the other two ghosts trailing behind her.

They rounded a corner into a familiar corridor, and Olive's ears perked up at the sounds of chatter and clanking silverware. When she stepped into the kitchen, despite her achy foot and itchy knees and stomach roaring with hunger, Olive smiled so hard it felt as though her face would split in two.

The entire cast of *Eidola* sat crammed, shoulder to shoulder, at the long table, which was covered in platters of roasted pheasant with buttery rice, fresh baguettes, and bowls filled with all kinds of fruit. On one side, Nadia the puppet was sandwiched between Aidan and Mickey. Mickey kept offering Nadia chunks of bread and pretending to be hurt when she didn't respond, sending Aidan into fits of giggles until his normally pale cheeks were beet red. Eli sat on Mickey's other side, deep in discussion with

Valentine across the table. Next to Valentine, Tanisha and Astaire were attempting to stack at least a dozen shiny red apples one on top of another. Juliana sat at the end of the bench, stuffing grapes in her mouth and snickering at the antics of Knuckles's hands: while the pianist himself floated peacefully at the end of the table, his severed appendages flitted here and there, doing karate moves on top of an unsuspecting Valentine's head and pretending to pick Aidan's nose, then wiping the findings on Mickey's sleeve.

This was a *real* family. And though the prospect was a little scary, Olive felt ready to be a part of it.

Juliana noticed her first and beamed, a half-chewed grape falling from her mouth. "Olive!"

"No, that's a *grape*," Mickey said exasperatedly. Then he glanced at the entrance. "Oh, *that* Olive!"

All conversation came to a halt as the others turned too. In the next second, Olive was overwhelmed with hugs and handshakes and pretend-nose-picking (until Knuckles shooed his left hand away from her face). Juliana grabbed her tightly by the wrist and led her to the table, and soon Olive was wedged between her and Astaire. The mime, who seemed overjoyed to see Olive, gestured emphatically at the food.

Olive didn't need any encouragement. She ripped off a huge chunk of baguette, piled her plate with pheasant and rice, and ate. And ate. And ate. Though the food was delicious, an odd taste lingered on Olive's tongue—musty, sour. A side effect of going well more than a day without eating, she decided, and crammed several orange slices into her mouth.

"Where did all of this come from?" she asked after swallowing.

"Eli cooked!" Val exclaimed. "It's been ages since he cooked for us."

"I can't remember the last time I had a meal like that," Tanisha said with a longing glance at the pheasant, and Olive saw that her plate was empty. In fact, the only ones actually eating were Juliana and Aidan. The others must have finished before Olive arrived.

"It's been ages since there was anything decent around here *to* cook," Eli was saying. "That's just how it is these days. But maybe the good times are coming back." He smiled warmly at Olive, and she felt her cheeks heat up.

"Dahling," Mickey purred in an impression of Maude so flawless it sent Tanisha into fits of laughter. "The seam-stresses found you sleeping on the lobby floor. You are aware we have beds, aren't you?"

"The door was locked," Olive said quickly. "The auditorium too. I couldn't get in."

"Why'd you come on a Monday, anyway? You know we don't rehearse." Juliana's eyes lit up. "Wait—are you here for good now? Are you staying?"

"Yes," Olive replied firmly. Juliana and Aidan cheered, but Olive noticed that the others exchanged sad glances.

Tanisha gave her a small, sympathetic smile. "What happened?"

Olive swallowed. "Nothing. I just . . . I'd rather be here."

Mickey started to respond, but Valentine silenced him with a look. "She doesn't have to tell us," they said. "All that matters is she's staying."

"It helps, though," Mickey insisted. "She'll feel better if she tells us. I know I did."

"Tell you what?" Olive asked nervously.

"Why you want to stay." Juliana grabbed an apple. "Not just be in the show but *live* here."

Olive thought of her father's empty study. She thought of Mrs. Preiss's flavorless soups, her constant nitpicking, her lack of faith. *You're simply not capable.*

"My mother . . . ," Olive began, and to her horror, her eyes welled up with tears.

"It's okay," Tanisha said hastily. "You don't have to tell us, not unless you want to."

"The important thing is we're happy you're here," Valentine added, reaching behind Astaire to pat Olive on the shoulder. "Maude will be thrilled."

Olive nodded gratefully, her gaze locked on the orange peels curled up on her napkin. Her throat was too tight to swallow food at the moment, so she just listened as the others shared their stories of how they'd come to Maudeville.

Mickey had liked drinks—the kind that made adults laugh too loud and do stupid things they claimed not to remember later. In Mickey's case, doing those stupid things had resulted in the loss of all the other things in his life that actually mattered. Valentine had graduated from medical school and promptly decided to become a magician instead of a doctor, which had angered their parents so much they hadn't spoken since. Tanisha suffered from frequent anxiety attacks after an incident in her childhood she preferred not to discuss, and found relief in performing. When it was Eli's turn to share, he simply said, "I wanted to fly," and everyone laughed and toasted him with cups of juice and coffee.

It was Aidan's story that startled Olive most. "I used to live with my aunt and uncle," he told Olive, helping himself to a handful of grapes. "We went to that big carnival last year in the park, and I got lost and never found them again."

"How is that possible?" Olive exclaimed. "The police couldn't help you?"

Aidan giggled. "I never went to the police, and I bet my aunt and uncle didn't either. They wanted to lose me, and I wanted to be lost." Olive stared at him, aghast, and he shrugged. "It worked out. I met a puppeteer at the carnival, and that's how I found Nadia. Then we found Maudeville."

Olive said nothing more, but Aidan's words stayed with her. She couldn't help wondering if Mrs. Preiss had gone to the police to report her daughter was missing. Or maybe she, like Aidan's aunt and uncle, would prefer things this way. Ripping the peel off another orange, Olive glanced at her hand. Her fingernails were caked with dirt from yesterday's adventure. No, not dirt. It was that glittery blue-green powder.

"I've noticed that too." Juliana's whispered words in her ear caused Olive to jump. She put her hands in her lap, embarrassed. But Juliana was examining her own fingers. "Look."

Olive leaned closer. Sure enough, the same stuff colored the whites of Juliana's nails.

"Weird, right?" Juliana shrugged. "I can't figure out what it is."

"It looks like Maude's eye shadow," Olive said.

Juliana snickered. "She does wear a lot of that stuff."

"But the last time it happened to me was when we were in here eating crackers," Olive added. "Maybe it's something in the kitchen." She rubbed the table experimentally. Her hand came away clean. The two girls surveyed the room—the brightly colored fruits in silver bowls, the platter of pheasant and rice, the silverware. . . .

"Tarnish!" Olive exclaimed. "That must be it. The knives and bowls are old. And look, the faucets too!" Eagerly, Olive grabbed a knife from where it lay next to a brick of cheddar. The silver glinted and gleamed, not a trace of tarnish to be found. "Well, not this one. But the others, I bet. That must be it, don't you think?"

"Must be," Juliana said, popping another grape into

her mouth. Olive wiped her fingers clean on a napkin and reached for a baguette just as Tanisha and Astaire's apple tower collapsed.

"Knuckles!" Tanisha exclaimed, shooing the pianist's left hand from an apple. "Get these things under control!"

"Sorry, can't," Knuckles said. "They're showing off for the seamstresses." Startled, Olive glanced up and realized that the three ghosts were still hovering in the doorway. Knuckles's right hand waggled its fingers at them, and the youngest ghost's shoulders shook in a silent giggle. The middle ghost, however, jumped in fright and zoomed straight up through the ceiling. With a weary look, the oldest ghost waved at Knuckles, then led the youngest out of the kitchen.

"Skittish, that Two," Knuckles said sadly.

"Two?" Olive repeated.

"That's what we call the seamstresses," Mickey explained. "One, Two, Three. One's the oldest."

"Why don't you call them by their names?" Olive couldn't help asking, and the fire-eater shrugged.

"We would if we knew 'em, but the seamstresses can't talk. Or they won't. Not sure which."

"And they can't mime, like Astaire," Juliana added. The mime sat up proudly, adjusting an invisible bow tie before taking a dainty nibble of cheddar.

"But they sure can sew," Mickey went on. "They made the cocoon, you know. That thing probably used up a thousand spools of thread."

Olive's eyes widened as she pictured the massive white prop hanging from the rafters. "It really is a cocoon? What's inside?"

"That's the best part of the show!" Aidan piped up, his lips stained red with strawberry juice. "A butterfly comes out during the finale. A *giant* butterfly. I haven't seen it yet, but I hear it flies out into the audience and everything."

"It does," Mickey confirmed. "It's incredible. My whole act changed after my first finale." Tanisha and Val nodded in agreement.

Olive ducked as Knuckles's hands flitted past, thumbs linked and fingers flapping like wings. She thought of Tanisha's floating rings and Astaire's invisible rope lifting her to the top of the boulder. She tried to picture a massive butterfly prop soaring over the stage, carried by ghosts. Then she frowned.

The youngest seamstress had tried to catch Olive when she fell, but Olive had passed right through her. The seamstresses could touch the needle and thread, though. Just like Knuckles's hands could play the piano.

"Knuckles," she said slowly, "how come your hands can't touch anything besides the piano?"

"Because they played it so much when I was alive," Knuckles said. "You know, before I lost them. At least, that's my theory." He gave her a friendly smile. "It's not like anyone gives you a manual on the rules of being a ghost when you die, you know?"

Chuckling, Eli held the platter of pheasant out to Olive. "There's plenty left," he said with a wink. Olive accepted another leg eagerly.

She had many more questions, of course. What about the ghosts who moved the props, who helped Eli fly and kept Tanisha's snow globes in the air and did the rest of the show's magic? Had they been aerialists and jugglers when they were alive?

But Knuckles was now preoccupied trying to get his hands away from where they were performing a kick-dance routine on Eli's shoulders. So Olive dug into her second pheasant leg and listened happily to the chatter of her fellow cast members. Yesterday's ordeal in her father's desk had been worth it, she decided. The penthouse was all but barren now, save for Mrs. Preiss. And a mother who looked right through you was worse than no company at all.

Maudeville was more than a theater now. It was home.

22
Troubled

The next few days were among the best of Olive's life. Rehearsals were more play than work; Olive drifted between *Eidola* the show and Eidola the place whenever the spotlight shone on her. She picked bouquets of snow-white lilies and collected golden leaves as they floated down from the treetops. She imagined an audience, and sometimes she even thought she saw them—every seat filled, all eyes on her. Then she'd blink, and they'd flicker and fade.

And she found herself more drawn to the cocoon with every rehearsal. Sometimes, when no one was looking, Olive would stretch to graze her fingertips along the bottom of it. Once or twice she thought she felt something stirring in the silk, and she wondered for the millionth time about the enormous butterfly inside. She couldn't wait for her first finale, when she would finally see it. Although as opening night drew closer, Olive found herself dealing with increasing nerves. She told herself the occasional bout of vomiting was something many performers probably experienced.

Olive hadn't seen any more new ghosts who might be contributing to the magic of the show, but she suspected she was starting to hear one. A sweet, distant voice occasionally joined her for a few lines, like an echo that harmonized her melody. No one else seemed to notice, but Olive suspected they heard the voice and chose to ignore it.

They'd moved on to Valentine's act, which was magic beyond anything Olive had ever witnessed. Valentine started by making the giant boulder prop vanish into thin air, and no matter how many times Olive watched, she could not see any evidence of mirrors or other trickery. Nor could she find the boulder backstage or hanging up in the rafters. It was as if the thing simply ceased to exist. A dozen enormous balloons bobbed overhead until a snap of the magician's fingers; then they dropped to the stage like lead, and Olive couldn't get them to budge. While she kicked and pushed, Astaire floated up as if filled with helium, and Valentine tied a string to his ankle so Olive could hold on to her mime for the rest of the act.

But the best part, in Olive's opinion, was when Valentine sawed Juliana in half. The girl climbed cheerfully into a rosewood cabinet just her size standing upright at center stage. Then Valentine would convince Olive to assist with the giant saw that cut through the cabinet—not across the middle, but *length*wise, starting at Juliana's head and moving down to her feet. Together, Valentine and Olive slid a set of panels in the center, then pulled the two halves apart and opened the doors just enough to reveal half of Juliana—one eye, half a smile, one arm, one waving hand. And though Olive knew it was just a trick, she simply didn't see how it was possible. It wasn't some sort of reflection, because Juliana's ponytail hung over her left shoulder and not her right. And the tiny mole was on her right cheek but not her left. Half of Juliana was on one side of the stage and half was on the other, and the sight both delighted and distressed Olive to no end.

"How does it work?" she asked Juliana eagerly. The two girls were huddled together offstage sharing a cup of water while the seamstresses repaired a tear in Valentine's billowing cape. Astaire floated peacefully overhead (he remained dutifully balloonlike until the very end of Valentine's act).

Juliana grinned. "Can't tell you. Val swore me to secrecy."

"Please," Olive pleaded. "Is it a mirror? Or is there a dummy that looks like half of you?"

"Nope!"

"Then what is it?"

"I told you, I can't . . ." Juliana's smile faded, her eyes locking onto something behind Olive. Turning, Olive watched One finish up Val's cape while Two and Three hovered nearby. And next to them . . . a flicker, a person-shaped shimmer.

"It's another ghost," Olive whispered, taking a step forward. But even as she squinted, the new ghost faded from sight. "Darn," she said. "I wonder if that's the one I've heard singing. Have you . . ." A choked sob cut her off, and Olive spun around in time to catch a glimpse of Juliana's long, dark ponytail before she disappeared through the side stage doors.

Olive was torn between running after her and trying to figure out the identity of the new ghost. Because she knew this must be the one Juliana had been talking to in the lobby—not Knuckles. Juliana had lied. This singing ghost was the one who had made her cry.

And Olive had a guess as to who the ghost might be.

With a worried glance at the stage doors, she hurried over to Val. The seamstresses smiled at her, and Three waved. Olive waved back.

"Val, did you see that ghost?" she asked. "Just a few seconds ago, right next to Two?"

Valentine was examining One's stitchwork on the tear in the cape. "Hmm? No, I didn't notice anyone."

"Do you ever see any ghosts other than the seam-stresses?" Olive pressed. Eli glanced over at them from where he sat on the edge of the stage, talking to Knuckles.

"There's this one here, don't know if you've met," he joked. Olive grinned halfheartedly as one of Knuckles's hands made a rude gesture over Eli's head. Eli glanced up and swatted at it. "Liang, I would've thought you'd have these things under control by now."

The pianist laughed. "Barely had control of them when

they were attached," he replied. "And Maude's the only person around here allowed to call me Liang—it's Knuckles to you, sir." When Eli rolled his eyes, Knuckles waved his arm at Val. "Hey, you call Valentine by their nickname! Why not me?"

"It's not my nickname," Val said dryly. "It's my name."

Knuckles grinned. "Not the one your parents gave you."

"True," Val agreed as One flitted around, giving the cape a final inspection. "I changed it."

"Was the name they gave you that bad?" Olive asked.

Val shrugged. "It was a perfectly nice name; it just wasn't for me. Like exchanging a shirt for one that fits better."

"I like your name *and* your shirt," Eli said, and Val smiled at him. Knuckles's hands slowly rose up behind Eli's head and curved toward each other with the thumbs touching to form a heart. Knuckles shooed them away hastily.

Olive cleared her throat. "Well, I think I saw another ghost just now. I've seen it twice, and both times Juliana got really upset."

A distinctly uncomfortable silence fell. Val and Eli exchanged a meaningful look, and Olive crossed her arms. She did not want to mention Finley—the cast always looked so distraught when anyone said the former star's name. But this was her home now too, and she deserved to know the truth.

"Please tell me who it is."

"Maudeville is filled with ghosts, Olive," Val said carefully. Eli fidgeted but said nothing.

"I know that," Olive replied with a touch of impatience. "Maude told me, and she said they're all nice. But I'm . . . I'm not so sure."

Val frowned. "What makes you say that?"

"Well, Juliana's obviously afraid of this one. And Felix is too."

"Felix?" Eli sat up straighter, eyes flashing. "You know him?"

Olive nodded. "He's always out in the alley. He's afraid to come in here, and he wants Juliana to leave. He says—"

"Stay away from him," Eli interrupted. Olive stared at him, confused and slightly hurt.

"Why?"

Eli started to respond, but Val silenced him with a look before turning to Olive.

"Felix is . . . troubled," they said slowly.

"So?" Olive retorted. "I am too. We all are. Maude said so herself—that's why we're here. If this ghost is so harmless, why can't Felix just come—"

"That boy is dangerous." Eli was on his feet now, spots of red visible beneath his beard. "Olive, listen to me. Do not bring him into this theater, under any circumstances."

And he walked off the stage, leaving Olive gaping at his retreating back. Val sighed, tightening the cape's ribbon around their neck.

"We need to get back to work" was all they said.

No one mentioned Felix for the rest of rehearsal. But Olive could not stop thinking about him and Juliana. Both of the Morellas were "troubled." Yet apparently, only one was welcome in Maudeville. Then there was the singing ghost, the one who made Juliana so weepy, the one the cast pretended not to see.

Olive knew deep down the singing ghost must be Finley. The former star of *Eidola* had died, and no one wanted to tell Olive how it happened. No one wanted to talk about why this ghost made Juliana cry or why it frightened Felix so badly he couldn't even step inside the theater.

And in all honesty, Olive wasn't sure she wanted to find out. But for the Morellas' sake, she had to try.

23
Never Leaving

That night, Olive couldn't fall asleep. Partly to blame was the churning in her stomach, no doubt caused by the cold leftover pheasant she and Aidan had indulged in before bed. She also hadn't yet gotten used to sleeping in a room with so many other occupants, especially occupants who sometimes mumbled (Eli), snored (Mickey), or fell off the bed in a great clatter of wood (Nadia). Olive listened as Aidan crawled down from his top bunk, gathered up his puppet, and laid her gently on the bottom bunk again before returning to his bed.

Olive closed her eyes, ribbons of flame still dancing behind her eyelids. She had seen Mickey's act for the first time that day. Dazzling and dangerous though all the fire fans and torches were, Olive couldn't stop thinking about Finley. She'd just begun to slide into an uneasy sleep when a muffled *click* startled her awake. She sat up in time to see someone slip out of the dorm.

Juliana.

Without hesitation, Olive threw aside her blanket and snuck out of the room. Her bare feet didn't make a sound as she tiptoed through the hall. Ahead, she saw Juliana's shadow just before it disappeared down the stairs. Olive followed, listening hard. On the last step, she heard a distant, familiar creak. She reached the backstage doors and slipped inside before they could close.

Olive stood in the dark, holding her breath and allowing her eyes to adjust. After a moment, she heard Juliana's shaky sobs on the other side of the curtain. Carefully, quietly, Olive crept closer.

"Please don't cry."

Olive froze. This was a new voice—a boy's voice. Olive fought the temptation to pull the curtain back, afraid of alerting the speaker and Juliana to her presence.

"But you look so . . ." Juliana's words were garbled with tears. "I can barely *see* you."

"But I'm getting better at controlling it," the boy said eagerly. "Like Knuckles, right?"

"He's been here for decades!" Juliana cried. "He's never leaving."

"Neither am I!" The boy sounded as though he meant the words in a comforting way, but Juliana moaned. "Don't you want me here with you?"

"Yes, of course. . . ." Juliana paused. "But I won't be

here forever. And it just feels . . . I mean, shouldn't you go wherever you're supposed to go when you're . . ."

"Dead?" the boy supplied, and Juliana burst into fresh tears. "Oh, I'm sorry! But, Juliana, I don't want to go anywhere else. And neither do you—you love it here!"

"I don't!" Juliana sobbed. "Not always. Sometimes I hate it here. Sometimes this place feels . . . wrong."

"Wrong?"

Olive couldn't breathe. Because she recognized the boy's voice now. But it couldn't be. It couldn't. Her fingers shook as she pulled the curtains open, just an inch.

Juliana stood there, tear-streaked and miserable, arms crossed as though she was trying to hug herself. And facing her was the faintest wisp of a person, the ghost of a boy with messy black hair and dark eyes.

His features blurred and flickered, and Olive tried to convince herself this was not Felix. Because Felix was not dead. She had seen him, very much alive and solid, on Monday when she arrived at the theater. He had tried to persuade her not to go in. And Olive had taunted him, asked why he wouldn't just come inside. Her stomach twisted as she remembered the last thing she said to him:

Are you really so afraid of ghosts that you'd just abandon your own sister?

A small cry of horror escaped Olive's lips. She clapped her hands to her mouth, but it was too late—Juliana spun around with a gasp. The Felix ghost stared at her curiously. Then everything went blindingly white.

"Ow!" Olive yelled, squinting and stumbling out of the spotlight. Neon spots danced in her vision, and she could just make out Juliana hurrying toward her.

"What are you doing here?" Juliana grabbed Olive and steadied her. "I . . ."

She stopped, and Olive rubbed her eyes hard. When she opened them, the Felix ghost was gone. In his place stood Maude.

"A bit late to be out of bed, isn't it?" Her voice was low and kind, but Olive felt Juliana shiver before she stepped forward.

"Yes, it's my fault." Juliana wiped her still-wet cheeks hastily. "I saw . . . I saw h–him again today, and I just had to . . . I needed to . . ."

"Oh, my poor dear." Maude shook her head and turned to Olive. "Darling, would you mind giving Juliana and me a little privacy?"

"Um . . ." Olive glanced helplessly at the miserable girl next to her, and Maude smiled.

"She'll be back to bed just as soon as we have a chat," she told Olive. "And we have a big weekend ahead, darling. You need your rest!"

At those words, Olive's eyelids drooped, and she yawned. Although a small part of her longed to stay and figure out what had just happened, her bottom bunk, with its scratchy sheets, suddenly sounded like the most wonderful place in the world.

So she obediently headed back to the dorm, promising herself she would stay awake until Juliana returned. But she drifted into a deep sleep almost right away. And when she woke in the morning, Juliana's bed was still empty.

24

A Familiar Boy

Olive sprinted to the kitchen without bothering to change out of her nightgown. Tanisha and Valentine were already at the table, and Eli stood at the stove, peering into a giant pot. Olive was just turning to leave when Aidan emerged from the pantry, followed by Juliana.

Stray strands of black hair had come out of her ponytail, and dark circles had formed under her eyes. She clung to Nadia tighter than seemed necessary while Aidan carried a box of oatmeal over to Eli. When Juliana noticed Olive, she dropped her gaze to the floor.

"I'm fine," she mumbled the moment Olive reached her side. "Don't ask."

"But—"

"Maude asked me not to talk about it," Juliana whispered, glancing up at last. The fear in her eyes sent a chill through Olive. With effort, she swallowed back her questions and followed Juliana to the table in silence.

Olive barely listened as Tanisha and Val chatted about

opening night on Saturday. Aidan joined them, sliding onto the bench next to Nadia. He glanced curiously from one girl to the other.

"What's the matter?" he asked, unfolding a napkin and placing it on Nadia's lap. Juliana started a little bit.

"Nothing," she said quickly. "I didn't sleep well, that's all."

"Me neither." The girls fell quiet as Eli set steaming bowls of oatmeal and banana on the table. Olive felt vaguely disappointed at having the same boring breakfast as she did at home. She noticed that Eli served only the children; both Tanisha and Val declined bowls before falling back into their conversation.

It took all of Olive's willpower not to bombard Juliana with questions about last night: Why did she tell the ghost she hated Maudeville? Was that really Felix? How had he died?

Her stomach churned with guilt. She had, after all, taunted Felix when he said he couldn't enter the theater. But apparently, Felix had had a very good reason for staying out in the alley. Somehow, coming inside had killed him.

Olive toyed with her spoon, wondering how she would possibly make it through rehearsal today. When she finally took a bite of oatmeal, she gagged.

Grabbing a napkin, Olive covered her mouth and pretended to cough. She spat the food out and wadded it up, then stared down at her bowl in disgust. The banana slices were rotten, coating the oatmeal in brown mush. The sickly-sweet taste lingered in Olive's mouth. She looked from Aidan, who was eating with gusto, to Juliana, who simply gazed at the table with a listless expression.

There must have been a rotten banana in the bunch, thought Olive. She didn't want to hurt Eli's feelings, so she waited a minute or so before standing and hurrying over to the sink, where she quickly scraped the foul, goopy stuff down the drain.

Even rehearsal wasn't quite enough to distract Olive from what she had seen last night. The acts were as spectacular as ever, the massive cocoon just as mysterious, the spotlight just as alluring. But just when Olive would start to lose herself in *Eidola,* she'd see a shimmer or hear a whisper and come to, glancing around for any sign of Felix's ghost. She couldn't stop thinking, too, of the singing ghost—*was* it Finley? What other secrets was Maudeville keeping from her?

When Maude asked her for a private chat after rehearsal, Olive's heart dropped.

"I'm sorry," she said the moment the last cast member had exited the stage. "I know I was off today. I'll do better."

Maude gave her a sympathetic smile. "Relax, darling. I wasn't going to chastise you. Saturday is opening night. A little stage fright is normal, particularly for your first performance."

Olive's hands twitched at her side. "It's not stage fright," she said quickly. "I'm just kind of distracted."

"Is something bothering you, dear?"

"Um . . ." Olive thought of Felix, of Juliana's teary pleas, of the singing ghost. She desperately needed to talk to someone about what was going on at Maudeville—and who better than Maude Devore herself? But something nagged at Olive. The way Juliana had shivered when Maude caught them onstage; the fear in the girl's eyes when she told Olive that Maude had asked her to keep quiet about Felix's ghost. *Sometimes I hate it here. Sometimes this place feels . . . wrong.*

"It's nothing," Olive said at last. "I just need to get some sleep."

"A wise idea," Maude agreed. "But remember, I'm here if you ever need to talk."

Under the stage lights, her teeth gleamed.

That night, Olive lay staring at the bunk above hers, where Juliana was curled up in a ball, sleeping—or pretending to sleep. Life at Maudeville did not come with much privacy, and Olive had not had a chance to talk to Juliana about Felix all evening. And while Juliana hadn't been avoiding her, Olive couldn't help noticing that she hadn't made much of an effort to talk to her either. Perhaps she knew, some-how, that Olive had taunted Felix about coming inside the theater. She might even blame Olive for the death of her brother. But Olive couldn't very well just ask Juliana about it in front of the other cast members.

So she had decided to ask Felix himself.

She waited until the rhythm of the snores and mumbles indicated that everyone was asleep, and then she slipped out of bed and into the hall. As Olive crept down the creaky stairs, a distant, lilting sound reached her ears. She froze, listening hard.

Someone was singing.

Heart in her throat, Olive hurried to the backstage doors and found them locked. She flew down the corridor and into the lobby and stopped in front of the entrance to the auditorium. The high, clear voice continued, and Olive recognized the opening number from *Eidola. Her* song. She pulled on the doors, expecting to find them locked as well. But they opened easily, and she stepped inside.

The auditorium was completely dark save for a single dim light. Not the spotlight—it radiated from a lamp that illuminated the stage with a soft, glowing circle. A lone, transparent figure stood in the center, the outline of the lamp clearly visible through him. Olive blinked in disbelief.

She moved slowly down the aisle, her eyes never leaving the ghost of a familiar boy with messy black hair. He did not seem to notice her presence; he was too wrapped up in his performance. But when she reached the stage as he held the last note, he opened his eyes and smiled at her.

"Hi, Olive."

25
First Finale

"Felix?"

Olive's voice came out as a tiny squeak. She shaded her eyes against the brightness of the lamp as she climbed the steps to join him on the stage. "Are you . . . how did you . . ." She trailed off, staring. Something wasn't right.

Up close, it was like looking at a slightly different version of Felix. The long, straight nose and dark hair were the same. But this boy's face was a touch rounder, his eyes wide with an innocence Felix didn't possess. Olive thought he might be a bit shorter too, but it was difficult to tell because he floated an inch or two off the ground. And his smile was . . . different. A nice smile. But different.

"Who are you?" she whispered. The boy straightened his back and lifted his chin.

"I'm Finley Morella," he told her. "I've been watching you since your first rehearsal. You're really good!"

Olive stared. Finley *Morella*?

"I miss singing, though," the boy went on, unaware of

Olive's shock. "I used to sing along with you, and it was okay because no one could see me or hear me. But now I'm getting more solid, and . . . well, you heard me the other day." He gave Olive a shy, apologetic look. "Kinda interrupted your performance. I think some of the other cast members heard me too, but they pretended not to."

A choked, croaky noise startled Olive. It was a moment before she realized it had come from her throat. Finley flickered and faded.

"Wait!" Olive stepped forward. "Don't go!"

Finley laughed. "Where would I go? Oh, that," he added, squinting at his translucent hands. "Hang on—watch this." Olive watched as he glided over to the boulder prop like a wisp of boy-shaped smoke. Finley knelt, prying at the trapdoor with his fingers. At first, they just slipped through the planks like vapor. But then, before Olive's eyes, the boy became more solid, more defined. The trapdoor trembled a bit, and his brow furrowed with concentration. At last, he pulled it open with a triumphant cry.

Olive could only gape. She could still see the boulder through him, but there was no denying that Finley was now a good deal more solid than he had been a minute earlier.

"It's because I was onstage so much," Finley explained, though Olive hadn't voiced a question. "It's easier to touch stuff I touched a lot when I was alive."

Olive thought of Knuckles and the piano, and the seamstresses with their needles and thread. She nodded wordlessly.

"I died on the boulder, I think," Finley went on matter-of-factly. "So I can touch it too. That's what I was trying to do when Juliana found me the other night." His smile vanished. "She cried again, just like the first time she saw me. I thought she'd be happy."

The first time she saw me. Olive pictured Juliana sobbing in the lobby, and her heart constricted. No wonder she'd been so upset.

"Are you Juliana's brother?" she whispered. "And Felix's?" When he nodded, Olive felt a tiny wave of relief. Felix was not dead after all.

But the former star of *Eidola* was, and while this wasn't a surprise, it wasn't exactly comforting either.

"Did you die during the show?" she couldn't resist asking.

"Yup." Finley sounded unconcerned, as if his onstage death had been nothing more than a lighting glitch. "The last thing I remember from being alive is the finale." His expression turned dreamy, and his features dimmed a tiny bit. "My *first* finale. It was a packed house—every single seat was filled. I was singing the last number, and the cocoon started to shake, and I was so excited because I'd never seen the butterfly, but everyone said it was just amazing. But then . . ." Finley frowned, concentrating. Then he sighed. "I don't know what happened next, just that I woke up in the trap room and I was dead."

Olive flinched. "I . . . I'm sorry."

"It's okay!" the boy said cheerfully. "It was frustrating at first because no one could see me except Maude. But she said if I wanted to stay, eventually everyone would see me again. And it's working!" His face fell. "I wish Juliana wasn't so sad about it, though. Felix keeps trying to get her to leave and join that carnival."

"Do you know why?" Olive asked. "Why he hates Maudeville so much?"

Finley shook his head sadly. "He did from the beginning. But he's just really protective, since he's the oldest. Felix was always trying to protect us from our dad. Running away was his idea, and Juliana and I followed him because . . ." Finley paused, making a vague gesture. "I don't know. We trusted him because he always took care of us. But we were hungry and sleeping on benches in the park, and . . ." His eyes brightened. "And then *I* found Maudeville. Maude said I could bring Felix and Juliana here and that we could stay and . . . and be safe." He sighed. "And Juliana loved it here as much as I did, but Felix . . . he just hated it, right from the start. He thought we were nuts for wanting to live here."

A shiver passed through Olive, and she rubbed her goose-pimply arms. "Yeah, he kept trying to tell me not to come here either."

"When Maude cast me in the show, Felix left," Finley said bitterly. "Maude told me and Juliana he was welcome back anytime. She was real nice about it. But Felix wouldn't even come inside the lobby." He paused, staring out into the auditorium. "He didn't even come see me when I died."

Olive swallowed. "Well, he wouldn't have been able to see you then," she pointed out, hoping to comfort him. "I can tell him you're visible now, if you want. I'm sure he'd come if he knew he could talk to you."

"No, that's not what I meant." Finley gestured to the open trapdoor. "He didn't come to the service."

"Service?"

Nodding, Finley floated down through the trapdoor. "Come see."

Olive cast a nervous glance around the auditorium, then followed. She gripped the ladder tightly, blinking as her eyes adjusted to the inky black beneath the stage.

"I guess I can't blame Felix for thinking Juliana's in danger, since I died and all," Finley said as Olive's bare feet touched the gritty ground. "But that was just an accident. She's a lot safer here than she was back at home," he added darkly. "Anyway, you'd think Felix would've at least come to say goodbye to me. Juliana's still mad he didn't."

It was so dark here, and Finley so barely visible, that it took Olive a moment to realize he was pointing to a lump of hard-packed dirt that glittered darkly like charcoal. A mound that was, in fact, roughly the size of a young boy. The truth ripped the breath from Olive's lungs.

This was where Finley's body was buried.

26
Radiant

The sight of the small, simple grave filled Olive with a rush of nausea. Her knees hit the ground, and through the sudden pealing of bells in her ears, she heard Finley's concerned voice fade to nothing. The incessant ringing stopped abruptly, and the world went mute. Her eyes darted around frantically, but the ghost was gone. It was just Olive, all alone under the stage with a body buried in the dirt.

Seized with panic, she flung herself at the ladder and began to climb, limbs quaking out of control. She pulled herself out of the trap room and blinked—the lamp was off, the blackness now absolute. Except . . . Olive's gaze fell on a sliver of dim light. The doors to the lobby.

Eyes glued to the exit, Olive climbed down off the stage. She moved as quickly as she dared down the aisle, bumping into armrests and scratching her legs. The silence was too complete, as if the theater were trying to convince her she was alone. It was the same feeling Olive had had back at the penthouse in the dead of night—invisible eyes peering through a crack in her bedroom door. She reached the exit at last, tore across the lobby, and burst out of the theater. Olive sprinted down the street, desperate to put as much distance between herself and Maudeville as possible. And then she stopped.

She stood there in the middle of the road, her back to the theater, taking deep, gulping breaths. Warm night air filled her lungs, the *everything* smell of the city comforting her, stars twinkling kindly overhead. Her terror at what had just happened had already begun to fade. She wasn't sure why she'd stopped running, exactly. But now she had the overwhelming sense that if she left Maudeville, she would never find it again. And despite everything she'd just learned, she wasn't quite ready to leave. After all, Olive reasoned to herself, she'd known from the start that the place was haunted.

Most of the city's theaters had their ghosts. And the ghosts Olive had met at Maudeville were perfectly nice.

Yet Olive couldn't turn around and walk back inside. Nor could she bring herself to walk away. She stood like a statue in the street, hit with a sudden urge to curl up on the gravel and sleep. A warm hand touched her elbow, and she shrieked.

"Sorry!" Felix took a step back, eyes wide. He started to say something else, but it turned to a cry of surprise when Olive threw her arms around him. After a few seconds, he hugged her back, although gingerly. Olive pulled away, too relieved by the presence of a living, breathing human being to feel embarrassed. And without waiting for him to ask, she told him everything.

Felix listened intently. When Olive reached the part about Finley singing onstage, his expression faltered. He squeezed his eyes closed as she explained that Finley couldn't remember exactly how he'd died but that Maude had encouraged him to stay. When she haltingly told Felix about the grave in the trap room, he made a small, fragile noise. He wiped furiously at his face, and Olive looked down, pretending not to notice his tears.

"He's happy here, though," she added hastily. "He said so, and he seemed like he meant it."

Felix rolled his eyes. "Yeah, I'm sure he is. He loved this place from the beginning, just like you."

Olive fidgeted. "Well . . . what's wrong with that? Knuckles and the seamstresses are happy here too."

"So that means they should stay here forever?" Felix asked sharply. "Stuck in some old theater?"

Olive didn't respond. In truth, she could think of far worse places to spend eternity. Felix let out a humorless laugh.

"You get the same look on your face as Finley did whenever you think about Maudeville," he told her. "I remember when he first told me and Juliana about this place—the way he described it, it might as well have been heaven. Then he brought us here and I thought he'd lost his mind. But

Juliana seemed to love it too, and I don't understand—"
His voice broke, and his jaw clenched. "Look at it, Olive.
Please, just turn around and look."

Dread crept up Olive's spine. "Why? I know what it
looks like. You've already—"

"You ran out here like the devil was chasing you," Felix
interrupted. "You were terrified. And not of Finley's ghost.
You were afraid of the *theater*. Look at it, before you forget."

At that moment, there was nothing Olive wanted to do
less. She couldn't explain it, not even to herself. She'd seen
Maudeville dozens of times. So why should it be so hard,
in this moment, to face it? Lifting her chin, Olive forced
herself to turn around. Her heart stammered in protest.

The beautiful, elegant Maudeville was gone. In its
place stood an abandoned theater, a condemned, hellish
place. The steps were crumbling, stiff brown weeds poking
through the cracks like corpses. Grayish mold clung to the
thick columns, and some sort of green-black grime coated
the once-glittering mosaic, forming sinister snake-eye pat-
terns across the facade. The doors stood slightly ajar, and
the darkness within seemed to move, as if it were a living
thing that could spill out, creep down the stairs and into the
street, and swallow everything in its path.

"It's evil," she whispered. "It's . . . wrong." She couldn't
tear her eyes from the horrific sight as she turned her
head slightly toward Felix. "Why did it change? *How* did
it change?"

"It didn't," Felix replied. "That's what it's always looked like. At least to me. The inside was even worse."

"But . . ." Olive couldn't accept what she was seeing. "When was the last time you went inside?"

His mouth was set in a thin line. "The night my brother died."

There was nothing to say to that, no adequate response. Comforting words, however well-meaning, disappeared into the void that opened up inside a person when a loved one was plucked from existence. Olive knew this as well as anyone, and so she said nothing and simply waited for Felix to continue.

"I kept looking for other options," Felix said quietly. "But it's hard, because I knew most places would just contact our father once they found out we were runaways. I'd spend all day trying to scrape up money, and Juliana and Finley would stay here. They kept going on and on about how perfect it was. And after a few weeks, I started thinking . . ." He sighed, casting a dark look at the theater. "I thought maybe I should just go see this show they were so excited about. Give it a chance, you know?"

Olive nodded, keeping her eyes fixed on his face. She felt as though the theater was glaring at her.

"I snuck in through the door in the alley," Felix continued. "When I walked into the hall, Finley was onstage, singing. He saw me, and . . ." He squeezed his eyes closed. "He just froze. I don't know why, but he looked like he was afraid of me, or afraid of—of something. After a few seconds, something grabbed me."

"What was it?"

Felix shook his head. "I don't know. I couldn't see anything. But it was strong. It grabbed me here"—he gestured to the back of his shirt, at his neck—"and dragged me backward through the lobby. But I heard Finley scream before it threw me out the doors. Finley screamed, and there was a crash, and then he . . . he stopped screaming."

Here his voice broke, and Olive felt his grief acutely. Or maybe it was her own anguish, a keen sorrow she'd done her best to keep locked up tight, that was breaking free at last.

"It was an accident," Olive heard herself say.

Felix snorted. "That doesn't make it any easier to deal with."

Privately, Olive disagreed. She tilted her head back and gazed at the night sky, trying to ignore the faint throbbing in her chest, the same old scar that never did quite heal right.

"Your mother is looking for you."

Olive snapped back to attention. "What?"

"I've seen interviews in the newspapers," Felix told her quietly. "She used to be famous, and now her daughter's missing. Reporters are all over her. She's got all kinds of people looking for you, flyers everywhere. She's offering a reward."

"So?" Olive said, her voice flat. "You don't think your father's looking for you?"

Felix's expression darkened. "He probably is. But not for the same reason as your mother."

"Which is what?" Olive couldn't help but ask, and Felix blinked.

"She loves you."

Olive laughed humorlessly. "That's just an act."

"I don't think so," Felix said. "She seems frantic. She said—"

"Don't," Olive whispered, staring at the pavement and willing the ground to stop shifting beneath her feet. It was a moment before she realized that the darkness from the theater was pooling around her feet.

She stumbled away, and Felix grabbed her arm. They stared at the long, long shadow, following it down the street and up the stairs and to the double doors, where Maude stood tall and smiling.

Light blazed from inside the lobby, casting a warm glow around the elegant woman. Squinting, Olive realized that the theater was beautiful once more, and she took an involuntary step forward. Felix tightened his grip.

"Don't," he whispered. "It's not real."

"Olive, sweetheart," said Maude, and her deep, soothing voice wrapped around Olive like a blanket. "I'm sorry Finley gave you such a fright. That was precisely why I told Juliana not to tell you about his ghost—I just didn't want you to be afraid, darling, especially since the rest of my cast is already so traumatized. It was my mistake, and I apologize. Please come back inside and I'll explain everything."

"Leave her alone," Felix said boldly, though Olive could feel his fingers trembling. "She doesn't want to be in your show anymore."

"You poor boy." Maude's wide, dark eyes locked onto Felix. "I am so sorry for your loss . . . although I would think you'd care enough about your sister to at least come and visit once in a while."

Felix made a disbelieving noise. "I can't! You know I can't—those doors won't open for me anymore. I've tried!"

Maude's lips quirked up. "My doors are always open, darling." She turned her attention back to Olive. "Everyone is free to come and go as they please. They are all here of their own free will—both the living and the dead. My theater is a sanctuary for those who cannot find happiness in the world outside these walls."

Olive pulled away from Felix, staring hard at the building that had looked so decrepit just minutes earlier. But she'd had a fright, and her mind had projected her fears onto the theater, tricking her into seeing wicked things lurking in the shadows. Now there was light, and light always showed the truth, didn't it?

The theater was *radiant*.

"Come with me," she told Felix. "Come inside and you'll see it's okay."

He groaned. "No, it's not. She's lying, Olive. You can't—"

But Olive had already tugged her arm from his grasp. She understood now why Felix couldn't open the theater doors. It wasn't Maude keeping him out, and it wasn't a fear of ghosts . . . although in a way it was. Felix's brother was dead, and he wasn't ready to face that reality yet. Like Juliana and the rest of the cast, Felix was grieving. He just had a different way of dealing with it.

"It's going to be okay," she told him quietly. "I'll come back out tomorrow, and the day after that. I'll come back out every day until you're ready to come inside with me."

"You don't understand," Felix protested, and Olive smiled sadly.

"I really do."

With that, she turned and walked toward the theater, up the grand staircase where Maude stood waiting patiently. They entered the brightly lit lobby together, the doors closing with a purposeful *click* behind them.

27

The Most Beautiful Place in the City

a troubled boy
such a shame
terrible tragedy
abandoned his sister
feels responsible
his brother's death
mustn't blame him
not ready to face reality
poor thing

Maude's words flittered around Olive's dreams like moths. Maude had explained the whole story to her last night— that Felix had burst in during a show and startled the cast, disrupting their focus and causing chaos. The horrifying result was that the great white cocoon had fallen, crushing Finley. His death was Felix's fault, and though it was an accident, it had marred Felix's view of the theater forever.

Olive had crept into bed long after the rest of the cast fell asleep. When she woke, the other beds were empty. Olive pulled on her robe and hurried to the kitchen.

Laughter and louder-than-usual chatter greeted her when she stepped through the entrance. She sought out Juliana first, seated in her usual spot at the end of the bench, near Knuckles. While the other cast members buzzed with excitement over opening night, Juliana was subdued. She hadn't been quite the same since that night on the stage with Finley. Olive squeezed in between Juliana and Astaire.

"Just in time!" Eli said, beaming at Olive and handing her a plate piled with piping-hot, fresh croissants.

Despite the delicious smell, Olive's stomach churned unpleasantly. She accepted one, hoping her nerves about opening night weren't returning. Closing her eyes, Olive tried to savor the buttery taste of the flaky roll. But that same odd tang was present, the one that lingered in the background of everything she ate. Maybe this wasn't nerves; maybe she was coming down with whatever Juliana had had a few weeks ago. Swallowing, Olive turned to ask her about it and froze.

Juliana was staring at her in horror, her croissant untouched on her napkin. And when Olive looked down at her own croissant in her hand, she dropped it with a small cry of disgust.

The girls stared at it in silence as the rest of the table chattered on, happily oblivious. It might have been a croissant once. But now it was a shriveled, wrinkled hunk all covered in greenish–bluish mold. Bile rose in the back of Olive's throat, and she clamped her hand over her mouth.

"Everything all right?"

Olive looked up to find Eli watching her closely. Across the table, Aidan cheerfully broke his croissant into smaller pieces to share with Nadia.

"It's good, right?" he said happily. "They're from the bakery just down the street. I got them this morning."

Olive nodded, unable to respond. Because now her croissant looked perfectly normal once more. Her eyes met Juliana's, which mirrored her fear and confusion. Olive could still feel the mold coating her teeth and tongue like slime, and she was gripped with the sudden knowledge that she was going to vomit once again.

In a flash, Juliana swatted her glass of juice, which splashed onto Olive's lap. "Oh, sorry!" she cried, pulling Olive to her feet. "Here, I'll help you clean this up." She pushed Olive out of the kitchen, down the hall, and into the bathroom just in time.

Nearly a minute later, Olive slumped against the wall next to the sink. The acidic, sour taste still lingered in her mouth. Juliana silently filled a cup of water from the faucet and handed it to Olive, who slurped it gratefully.

"You're hallucinating too," Juliana said, sitting cross-legged across from Olive. "I got sick like that last week. It's been getting worse for me, ever since . . . um . . ."

"Finley," Olive croaked, and Juliana nodded. "What else do you see besides rotten food?"

Frowning, Juliana picked at a chip in the tiled floor. "Just, like . . . dirt. Grungy stuff, like the place hasn't been cleaned in a long time. Bugs sometimes. And . . ." She trailed off, shifting uncomfortably. "I don't know. That's it, I guess."

So Olive told her what she'd seen last night—the way the whole outside of the theater had looked condemned. Juliana squeezed her eyes closed as if she was trying not to cry.

"That's how Felix always said it looked too," she whispered. "Why? Why does it look like that to him but so beautiful to the rest of us? What's wrong with him? What's wrong with *me*?"

Olive knew the answer. But she didn't want to say it. "Juliana," she said hesitantly. "That night you were with Finley's ghost on the stage, and you talked to Maude after I left . . . what did she tell you?"

Juliana's expression closed. "Why?"

"Because . . ." Olive couldn't find the words. "Felix can't come inside, and . . ."

"He *won't* come inside, you mean!" Juliana's face was red now, her eyes brimming over. "Because he feels too guilty about—" She stopped, clapping her hand over her mouth.

But Olive understood. "He caused the accident," she said.

Juliana nodded slowly. "How did you know?"

"Maude told me last night."

"She told me too, that night on the stage."

Olive frowned. "You didn't see it happen?"

"No." Juliana rubbed her face. She suddenly sounded exhausted. "I was in Val's vanishing cabinet. All I know was by the time they finally let me out, the cocoon had already . . ." Her voice broke. "No one even wants to talk about Finley anymore, like he never existed."

"They just don't want to upset you," Olive pointed out.

Juliana rolled her eyes. "Like not talking about something means it never happened," she muttered. "I *want* to talk about Finley. I miss him so much."

Olive said nothing. For Felix, grief was best kept behind a closed door. But Juliana needed the door open. Olive wanted to explain this, but in a way that wouldn't make Juliana even more upset. They sat in silence for a few minutes. Olive sipped at her water. It burned going down her raw throat.

"Felix says he *can't* get into the theater," she told Juliana at last. "I think it's for the same reason he sees it as being ugly." She thought of Maude's words. "He can't face the reality of it. Of Finley's death."

Juliana's lips trembled. "Maybe that's why I see it as ugly too sometimes."

"Maybe," Olive agreed.

"But wait." Juliana frowned. "Felix *always* saw it as

ugly, even the very first time Finley brought us here. That doesn't make sense."

"You and Finley never thought it was ugly?"

"Oh no," Juliana said emphatically. "It looked old, but in a beautiful way, you know?"

Olive did know. It was exactly how she'd seen it the first time too. And every other time, save for last night, and the night she'd run away. Felix was the only one who always saw the theater the wrong way.

The girls jumped when the door swung open. Tanisha peeked inside, her eyes widening when she saw them on the floor.

"Everything okay?" she asked. "You've been gone awhile."

"Fine," Olive said quickly, pulling her knees in to hide the juice stains she hadn't bothered rinsing out of her robe. "What are those?" She pointed to the stack of papers in Tanisha's hand.

"Programs for tomorrow night!" Tanisha held one up. "Pretty exciting, right?" Olive's breath caught in her throat when she saw the cover.

EIDOLA

STARRING OLIVE PREISS

"Wow," she said, her voice higher than usual. Tanisha beamed.

"Better change out of that robe before dress rehearsal."

Nodding, Olive got shakily to her feet. Dress rehearsal. Opening night. *Eidola,* starring Olive Preiss.

"Do you have anyone coming tomorrow night?" Tanisha asked. "Any family?"

"No," Olive replied distantly. "No, I don't have anyone."

She allowed Tanisha and Juliana to lead her to the dressing room, where the seamstresses were waiting. Two, shaking with either nerves or excitement, floated over to Olive with her costume: a long, flowing nightgown with ribbons and a high waist. They fluttered around her, hemming and making adjustments, and Olive gazed at herself in the gilded mirror as they worked. She felt better than she had in days, though her stomach still roiled unpleasantly. The Morellas needed help, and Olive had an idea. She would make Felix understand that he couldn't blame himself for his brother's death. She would make him see that Maudeville was the most beautiful place in the city, and reunite him with his brother and sister.

The seamstresses fussed over her as she plotted and schemed, clenching her hands into fists to hide the blue-green smudges still on her fingers.

28
Worth the Wait

Dress rehearsal proved to be the perfect escape from all of the day's earlier unpleasantness. From the moment the spotlight beamed down on her, Olive was transported. It was as if the seats had vanished and the walls and ceiling retracted and she was alone, truly alone, until Astaire rescued her and brought her to a land filled with flying glass globes and sparkling snowflakes, soaring angels and devilish fire-eaters. Boys swapped souls with puppets, and girls could be sawed right down the center, then come back together with a laugh and a bow. Magic was real.

Olive sang with her head tilted up to the heavens. Out of the darkness, the shimmering white cocoon descended lower and lower. It glowed faintly, and Olive felt a light pulsing behind her eyes in response. There was something beautiful in there, a glorious butterfly with wildly colorful wings that could take her anywhere, anywhere at all. Olive was ready. She would go wherever the butterfly took her.

And then, quite suddenly, she was no longer in Eidola. Just a theater.

Blinking, Olive looked around as the house lights came on. The other cast members seemed dazed, too, though most were smiling. Aidan rubbed his eyes, then gently lifted Nadia, who'd toppled over at his side. "Aw," he said. "Still no butterfly?"

"Saving it for tomorrow night," Mickey replied. "That's only for the live performance."

Maude ascended the stairs, her smile wider than ever. "Exactly right. That was magnificent, everyone. Just beautiful." Her glittering eyes were fixed on Olive, who shivered with pleasure at the praise.

But for the first time, a small part of her was disappointed. Escaping to a fantasy world onstage wasn't quite enough anymore. She gazed at the glowing cocoon, part of her still willing whatever was inside to emerge and take her away.

"Tomorrow night." Maude's whisper tickled Olive's ear, causing her to jump. "It will be worth the wait, I promise."

"I know," Olive said. Her wide, wide smile mirrored Maude's.

Before dinner, Olive slipped out of the theater and peered down the alley. She looked everywhere, even in the dumpster, but Felix was nowhere to be found.

Olive had been expecting that, and so she'd written

a note in one of the *Eidola* programs. She hemmed and hawed for several minutes over where to leave it: sticking out from under the dumpster, tucked under the lid, lying on top of the least filthy trash bag inside. At last, she placed it on top of a slightly smashed pink bakery box, using an apple core as a makeshift paperweight. It would have to do.

She closed the lid and headed back into Maudeville, humming under her breath.

29
Forgotten

Sleep did not come until very late that night. The cast, still buzzing with adrenaline after rehearsal, filled the dorm with chatter and laughter into the small hours. Someone had unearthed a record player, and the scratchy vinyl sound of tinny brass harmonies and rapid drum rhythms provided a soundtrack to the impromptu festivities. The music reminded Olive of better times, when her still-happy father would come home from work, throw down his briefcase, put on a jazz record, and dance clumsily around the living room with Olive standing on his feet. The memory fit the music—mostly joyful, but with the mild ache of longing.

Olive and Juliana sat cross-legged on Olive's bed with Finley floating overhead, trading jokes with Aidan and cheering when Mickey led Nadia around in a waltz. Tanisha helped Val do their hair into an elaborate braided coil, and Astaire played a silent yet violently energetic game of poker with Knuckles's hands. Eli sat on the floor, knees tucked up to his chin, watching the others with a wistful sort of smile.

"This is my favorite part," he told Olive when he caught her staring. "The night before opening night."

Olive smiled and shook her head. Nothing could be better than opening night, putting on an amazing show for a rapt audience, bringing *Eidola* to life.

But looking around the dormitory at her new family all laughing and celebrating, she thought maybe she understood what Eli meant. This *was* life, no magic or acting or pretending required. This was real.

The thought comforted her and made her sad at the same time.

Finley had more or less mastered staying visible, and the others had welcomed him back as if he'd returned from a trip to the beach rather than the dead. And though Juliana was clearly happy to have her brother by her side, Olive could tell she was still frustrated by the way everyone was behaving. The rest of the cast was acting as though nothing horrible had ever happened, as if there was no reason to grieve now. They did not discuss Finley's onstage death even once, and Finley was too polite to bring it up.

Several times, Olive almost told Juliana and Finley about the note she'd left for Felix. But then Astaire would duck and cover as Knuckles's hands flung their chips at him, or Tanisha would try to teach Aidan to juggle shoes, or Mickey would sweep Val into a rather wild tango, and there would be more laughter, and Olive would momentarily forget. At last, she decided it would be best not to tell Juliana or Finley. That way, they wouldn't be disappointed if Olive's plan didn't work out.

And if it did, opening night would be a family reunion too.

Despite the late night, Olive woke early the next morning. She groped around her satchel for a fresh pair of socks but instead pulled out a book. *The Cabinetmaker's Apprentice.*

The scar in her chest throbbed again, more intensely than ever. Olive had barely thought of her mother in days. It hadn't even been intentional. Her mother's sharp gaze and harsh words had simply ceased to exist in Olive's mind. This frightened her, both because she didn't want to remember and because she didn't understand why she had forgotten so easily and so quickly.

Her hands shook as she fumbled with the book, eager to stuff it back into her satchel and out of sight. Something slipped out from between the pages: a rectangular slip of paper with the words *Laurel Preiss* written in careful, bold print in the center. It was not her mother's handwriting. Beneath that, the same hand had noted a sum of money: *Fifty-two dollars and* 40/100 *cents.* A signature Olive couldn't decipher was scrawled in the bottom right corner. On the top left, a typed address: *Kay's Laundry and Tailor Service.*

Olive's mother used to write a check made out to Kay's once a month before she'd been forced to give up such luxuries. But this check wasn't *from* Mrs. Preiss. It was *to* her. Memories flooded Olive's mind: long days alone in the penthouse; raw pink calluses on her mother's fingers.

Mrs. Preiss was cleaning other people's clothes, mending their shirts, getting stains out of their linens. She had gotten a job, a job that didn't involve singing. And now she was talking to reporters, putting up flyers, offering rewards for her daughter's safe return. *She seems frantic,* Felix had said. *She loves you.*

Emotions Olive did not want to feel welled up inside her anyway, her old life suddenly pushing at the dam she'd unknowingly built, threatening to overflow. She crammed the check back in the book, shoved the book into the bag, and threw the bag onto the floor. Across the room, Tanisha cried out in alarm. Mickey's snores ended abruptly, and Nadia fell off her bed in a clatter.

"Sorry!" Olive squeaked, her heart pounding painfully. "I . . . dropped something."

Juliana's upside-down head appeared in front of her, long ponytail dangling as she hung over her bunk. "You okay?"

"Yup!" Olive couldn't get her voice back to normal. "Just excited about tonight, I guess."

Juliana grinned. Her smile was upside down too.

"Same here."

30
Its Own Kind of Magic

Breakfast was a rowdy affair. Lack of sleep had done nothing to subdue the cast members' moods. Their enthusiasm was contagious, and Olive tried to put the check firmly out of her mind as she ate a few bites of a slightly stale bagel.

The day stretched on too long and too warm. Olive was desperate for a distraction. Every time she closed her eyes, she saw her mother scrubbing stains out of strangers' clothes, and guilt jabbed at her insides. She played cards with Aidan and wandered around the lobby with Juliana. She skipped lunch and pretended to take a nap instead. She wasn't hungry.

She wasn't tired either.

At last it was time to get ready. Olive stood perfectly still as the seamstresses fussed over her once more, thread flying as they hemmed and stitched. She smiled at Two and received a kind, if anxious, smile in return. When the seamstresses finished, Olive thanked them and left the dressing room. The rest of the cast was backstage, but she did not join them—not yet. Instead, she hurried down the stairs and through the hall. After a furtive glance around to make sure she was alone, Olive quietly pushed the side entrance open and stepped out into the alley.

No Felix.

Deflated, Olive leaned against the door. Maybe he hadn't gotten her note. Or maybe he had, and he'd chosen not to come. Maybe, Olive thought forcefully, Juliana was right. Maybe Felix simply wasn't a very good brother.

She turned to head back inside and spotted a rusted barrel next to the dumpster. Then, without giving herself a chance to change her mind, she dragged it over to the side entrance. Stepping inside, Olive allowed the door to close. It rested on the can, leaving an opening wide enough for anyone to notice.

She headed down the hall, satisfied. Felix could still come to the show if he changed his mind. He could see his sister and brother again. It was his choice.

Olive was greeted backstage with a rush of *good luck*s and kisses on the cheek and pats on the back from her fellow cast members. Their excitement was like an electric current, a charge that crackled and sparked and made Olive's skin tingle and her heart beat faster. Opening night had its own kind of magic. Olive wondered briefly if this was how her mother had felt before her big performances. Then she shook that thought off.

She took her spot in the pit, listening to the crowd on

the other side of the closed curtains. It wasn't the obnoxious chatter punctuated with coughs and high, false laughter Olive typically heard when she attended a show. This was a gentle flutter of almost reverent-sounding whispers . . . and occasionally, what sounded like a muffled sob or soft moan of fear.

The hair rose on the back of Olive's neck, and she leaned forward. But then the whispers fell silent, the house lights dimmed, and the curtain rose. Olive squinted out at the hall as the first piano chords sounded. It wasn't until the spotlight hit that she forgot about the audience completely.

Eidola had begun.

31

An Intruder

Olive gave herself over to the show. She sang her sad, sweet song in the pit, her voice breaking with emotion as she thought of how long she had been abandoned, alone. Astaire had made her laugh for the first time in what felt like years. But now his flailing dancing and whimsical gestures reminded her of old films on lazy Sunday afternoons, and the scar in her chest was getting too painful to ignore.

They emerged from the pit, and *Eidola* took Olive's breath away, just as it had the first time. Each act was spectacular, every performance flawless. It really was, as Maude had promised, the most incredible show in the city.

But it was still just a show. And that wasn't enough anymore.

The more Olive sang, the more she never wanted to leave Eidola. She desperately wanted everything else—the stage, the seats, the still-aching scar in her chest—to disappear. And then this dreamland, this magical place, would be her new reality. Her lungs ached as she poured that hope into the finale, her first finale, surrounded by streaks of fire and flurries of snow. Mickey's torches were a fiery blur, battling with Tanisha's flashing silver rings. Val invited Juliana into the vanishing cabinet while Nadia cheered and Aidan watched with a wooden smile. And Eli twisted and flipped so impossibly high in the air. It was all beautiful. It was perfect.

Until an intruder arrived.

He slipped into their fantasy world like a shadow, one that Olive pretended not to see at first. She stood on the edge of a great cliff, surveying her new home, surrounded by her new family, singing beneath the blindingly bright sun. The shadow crept through the golden forest and crossed the frozen lake. He stood at the bottom of the cliff and gazed up at Olive, and he was no longer a shadow but a boy. A boy who did not belong in her Eidola.

"Look," yelled Felix, and he held up a piece of paper.

Olive's voice faltered. She took a step back from the edge of the stage—no, it was a cliff—and squeezed her eyes closed.

"Go away," she hissed. A moment later, a hand seized her wrist and pulled her down.

"I called," Felix said. "I told them where you are." He held out the paper again, and Olive's mind went blank.

Her own black-and-white face dominated the page, beneath the header *MISSING*. Olive recognized the picture as her school photo from last year. Below were her name, her age, and a number to call with any information on her whereabouts.

"You what?" It came out as a whimper, inaudible over the orchestra. Neon spots danced in her eyes as the spotlight burned brighter than ever. The spotlight, not the sun.

She heard the crowd's cheers now as they rose to a roar, drowning out the music. And then, just as quickly, faded to nothing.

The invisible orchestra honked and sputtered to a halt, Knuckles's hands stubbornly jabbing out one or two more disjointed chords. Olive heard a few noises from the cast behind her—a cry, a thud, a surprised curse—but she did not turn to look. Her eyes were locked on Felix's. He didn't look amazed or even embarrassed that he'd just brought *Eidola* to a screeching halt.

He looked like he pitied her.

"Turn around, Olive," he said quietly.

Just as on the other night out on the street, a feeling of dread slithered up Olive's spine. It was going to happen again. Her mind was going to trick her into seeing something else. Something wrong.

She vowed not to believe whatever she saw, and slowly turned around.

The rest of the cast stared at her blankly. Their costumes, so resplendent moments earlier, were tattered and dirty. Their props were just junk from the dumpster: rusted hoops, a scorched tiki torch, an old wardrobe with the left door missing. They blinked heavily, disoriented, squinting at one another and out at the empty seats, many of which were broken or torn. Olive looked down at herself in her mended but grimy nightgown, then back at the cast.

But they weren't a cast at all. Just a group of sad runaways with no home. Tramps playing make-believe onstage in a seedy, dilapidated hall. The truth sank into Olive as sharp as fangs.

This was the reality. Eidola had always been the illusion.

"You were right," she whispered. Her throat ached as she faced Felix again. "None of it was real."

Felix smiled in relief, but only for a second. Olive had the briefest glimpse of his eyes widening in horror before some invisible force yanked him, dragged him—not just away but *up.*

He flew higher and higher like a rag doll thrown by an angry toddler, all the way into the dome. Screams and shouts filled the air as the others watched, horrified, while Felix flailed and kicked. For a heart-stopping moment, they waited for him to plummet.

But his hands gripped the chipped bronze edge, and he dangled from the dome, legs pumping uselessly. Then the other cast members were yelling, moving, jumping off the stage, positioning themselves beneath Felix as if to catch him.

He's going to fall, Olive.

Something was prying its way out of the hole in Olive's

chest, deliberately popping her careful stitches one by one with its claws, exposing the infected wound. Something with a deep, soothing voice. But its words were anything but a comfort.

He's going to fall, and there's nothing you can do.

Nothing she could do. Felix scrambled for a better grip. The others were screaming, sobbing. Nothing she could do.

Just like last time. Isn't that right, Olive?

Olive turned around. She couldn't bear to watch it happen. The seamstresses had floated onto the stage and were gazing up at Felix in horror. Two covered her eyes with her hands. Olive could see the cocoon straight through her.

She'd been so sure the ghosts had been her invisible strings, helping her and Astaire and Eli to fly. But she'd fallen right through the seamstresses. They couldn't touch humans; they could only touch needle and thread.

Thread.

Olive cried out as if the idea had physically hit her. "The thread!" she screamed, sprinting to the cocoon. The seamstresses stared in confusion as she picked off a strand and ran toward them. "The cocoon is made of thread!" Olive thrust it at One, who took it with wide eyes. "There's tons of it—bring it up there, and . . . and wrap him up, carry him down!"

One's face lit up, and she zoomed off without hesitation. Two and Three followed, the thread unraveling from around the massive cocoon behind them. Olive hurried to the edge of the stage, hands pressed to her mouth. Nausea rolled over her as she watched Felix writhing so high above the ground, struggling to keep his grip. The seamstresses zipped around him, wrapping him like spiders would a fly. But not fast enough. The voice inside her chuckled.

He's going to fall, Olive. Just like your father.

32

Her Father

The stitches were popping fast, the hole ripping open. Unraveling just like the cocoon.

It was a long, long way down, wasn't it? Nine floors.

"Stop," whispered Olive. The voice was familiar now, deep and soothing. She didn't want to hear this voice say these things.

Right off the fire escape, splat *on the street.*

She couldn't see Felix's face from here, but she could hear his terrified screams. He was going to fall, just like her father.

But your father didn't fall. *Did he? Did he, darling? No. He*

jumped.

33
Burst Free

There was a desperate cry when Felix plummeted, surrounded by the frantic seamstresses. They yanked at the threads, tugging him into a spread-eagle position, straining to keep him in the air. But their efforts only slowed his fall. He landed with a sickening *crunch* somewhere in the middle of the sea of seats, and the other cast members scrambled to reach him. Olive remained onstage, paralyzed with fear and dread until someone shouted:

"He's okay!"

The auditorium went black.

A split second later, the spotlight blazed on Olive. She covered her eyes, tears mixing with sweat on her palms. A noise began behind her. A soft but powerful noise, like something very, very big trying to be very, very quiet. Lowering her hands, Olive turned around.

The great white cocoon was shifting, quivering. As Olive stared, the tremble turned to a shudder, and then it was thrashing violently. *Run, run, run!* her brain screamed, but when she turned and stepped out of the spotlight, she froze.

Shapes filled the seats, wisps of people with hollow eyes and black mouths stretched in silent screams of terror. When the massive cocoon fell to the stage with a *boom,* the shapes rose from their seats as one, soaring up and vanishing into the darkness of the dome.

Olive staggered away as the threads began to split, faster and faster until the cocoon ruptured and the thing inside burst free. But this was not a butterfly. Like the rest of the once-beautiful theater, this was *wrong*. Something with a gaping, toothless maw and no eyes. Something coated in darkly glittering grime and radiating the smell of earth and decay.

A colossal worm rose high above Olive, thread pooling around its slimy body. Then it dove, and she was swallowed in darkness.

34
The Trap Room

Death felt like a hug.

Olive lay very still, listening to the muffled shifty sounds and distant screams of terror. She knew she must be in the worm, but it didn't feel unpleasant. It felt like someone had wrapped a pair of arms around her and was squeezing tightly. Also, there was no slime. She was bone-dry.

"That's odd," she said out loud. And someone's breath tickled her ear.

"Shh!"

Olive gasped and lurched away, but the arms—real arms, human arms—only tightened around her.

"Don't move," Felix whispered. So Olive did not. The darkness was still absolute, but she realized they were lying on the stage. The worm was not. It was thrashing blindly around the auditorium, uprooting seats and smashing into walls. The screams had faded, and Olive could only hope the other cast members had made it to the lobby.

A sudden soft light made her blink. Quietly, carefully,

Olive and Felix pulled themselves apart and sat up. A lamp had appeared just over the trap-room door, illuminating the piles of thread. And floating faintly next to the lamp was Finley.

He smiled a wobbly smile at his brother. "Hi."

Olive glanced at Felix and then quickly looked away. It was too painful, his expression. As if a hole he'd stitched up inside himself was unraveling too.

Gong!

The worm crashed through the orchestra pit right behind them, and Olive tensed, ready to run. They made an easy target here on the stage in the light. But Finley held his hands out to stop her.

"It's blind," he whispered. "And deaf. It senses movement. Don't move."

So Olive stood still. The worm slithered slowly, pressing its massive body against the stage, close enough that she could smell the stench of decay again. As her eyes adjusted to the dim light, Olive noticed that the piles of thread weren't all that was left of the cocoon. Other objects littered the stage.

Bones. Skulls.

"You were right," Finley told his brother, and Olive forced herself to focus. "You were right the whole time about this place. It's all my fault for bringing us here."

"No." Felix's voice was fierce. Olive flinched—what if Finley was wrong about the worm being deaf?—but the thing just continued to slide behind them at a glacial pace. "It's my fault. I'm the oldest. I should have—" His voice broke. "It's my fault."

"It's not," Finley insisted. "When I was watching the show, I remembered everything that happened during my finale. I was singing, and all of a sudden you were there in the aisle. And when I saw you, the theater . . . it changed. All the magic was gone."

Olive shifted, and the worm paused. The three of them fell silent, still as statues, until it began to crawl again.

"Then *she* grabbed you and dragged you away," Finley went on in a hushed voice. "So I started screaming and screaming, and then that thing . . ." He gestured to the piles of thread that remained of the giant cocoon. "It fell on me." Finley floated closer, his expression earnest. "It wasn't your fault, Felix. It really wasn't. It was *hers*. But when I woke up in the trap room, I'd forgotten. My memories were invisible, like the rest of me."

Olive wanted to ask who *she* was, but didn't. Because she knew.

"She saw you coming tonight," Finley told Felix, his mouth trembling again. "And she—she took Juliana. I was looking for her when I heard the worm."

"What?" Felix stepped forward, and Olive grabbed his arm. Her pulse raced out of control. "Juliana—is she . . ."

"In the trap room." Finley pointed at the door beneath his floating feet. "Alive," he added quickly. Olive's shoulders slumped with relief. "That's where she goes when she gets in Val's vanishing cabinet."

Felix shook his wrist from Olive's grip. "We have to get her out of here." He knelt down and began feeling around the edges of the door, looking for the latch. Olive moved over—cautiously, quietly—to help, and Finley joined them. His transparent fingers found the latch first, and soon they'd pried the door open. Below was nothing but black. Olive's heart ached as she thought of Juliana stuck down there in the dark with her brother's grave.

"Hurry," Finley said, before drifting through the stage. Felix and Olive looked at each other. Neither made a move.

The slithering had stopped.

Frozen in fear, Olive kept her eyes locked on Felix's. For a few painful seconds, everything was mute. Then:

Crash!

The massive thing slammed down inches from them, smashing the lamp, sending the bones of its previous meals flying, and plunging the auditorium into darkness. Olive groped blindly until her hands found Felix, and she shoved him through the trap-room door. She had just flung her legs over the side to follow when the worm's slick, slimy mouth closed around her. There was a tug on her feet, the world tilted, and Olive fell.

35

Abandoned

The impact of the landing knocked the wind out of her. She gasped for breath, too terrified to open her eyes.

"It can't get down here," came Finley's voice. "It won't fit." Olive heard the worm slam down on the stage overhead. She sat up, her head spinning. Next to her, Felix struggled to get to his feet. Olive used the ladder to pull herself upright. She felt eyes watching her from the shadows.

"Felix?"

Felix's head snapped up, and he and Olive glanced around for the source of this new voice. Olive saw her eyes first, shiny and scared. Juliana stepped forward with her arms crossed tightly over her chest. Strands of hair had come loose from her ponytail, and they clung to her sweaty, dirt-streaked face. For a moment, she and Felix simply stared at each other with mirrored expressions of fear and relief. Then Juliana launched herself at her brother.

They clung to each other, sobbing and choking out apologies while the ghost of their younger brother watched with the smallest, saddest smile Olive had ever seen. She turned away because this was a private family moment. But for another reason too. Right now, the Morellas only had eyes for each other.

But Olive still felt eyes watching *her*.

She turned slowly on the spot, looking, listening. The thrashing above had stopped. But something—someone—was down here with them. Olive searched the surrounding gloom for the source of the prickling on her neck. There, in the far left corner.

A glint of white teeth.

"Hello, darling."

Her husky voice seemed to come from all directions. She didn't move, but her other features gradually became more visible in the shadows. Glittering eyes, scalpel-sharp cheekbones, red lips stretched wide to reveal so many teeth. Olive heard Juliana gasp behind her, and Felix made a noise like an angry dog.

"That really was quite a show," Maude Devore said admiringly. "You were so perfect for *Eidola,* Olive. Just as I knew you would be."

She moved forward noiselessly. Fear ripped through Olive, but she planted her feet and spread her arms like a barricade to protect the Morellas. Maude had damaged their family enough. Olive would not let her hurt them again.

"I told you this theater burned once," Maude said,

gesturing up at the stage. "The fire began during the first act. I climbed down here to escape the smoke."

She stopped steps from Olive. The scent of dirt and decay hung between them, heavy and stifling.

"You remember how I discovered Eidola, don't you?" she asked quietly. "All those lonely hours I spent as a child, locked away. I created an escape. And once again I needed that fantasy. Because the theater trapped me down here, kept me safe from the fire." Maude paused, her gaze never leaving Olive's. "And I never left."

Olive shivered as Maude drew closer, inch by inch, and then

passed

through

her.

Heart hammering in her ears, Olive spun around and met the wide-eyed, frightened faces of the Morellas. No Maude.

"My apologies." Maude had reappeared next to Finley's grave. She brushed her skirt off. "I usually find such tricks rather juvenile, but they *are* hard to resist sometimes."

"Go," Olive breathed, pushing Juliana toward the ladder. "Go, we need to go. . . ."

Tears streaming down her face, Juliana began to climb. Finley floated up at her side, but Felix hesitated.

"Hurry," Olive whispered, and after a moment, he followed his sister.

Olive kept her eyes on Maude as the others made their way up slowly in the dark. She put her hand on the rung the moment Felix's feet cleared it. Maude shook her head.

"Oh, Olive, sweetheart," she said. "Do you really think you can leave?"

"Yes." Olive tried to keep her voice steady. "You said so. You said everyone is here because they choose to be. And I—I don't choose to be here anymore."

For the first time, anger flashed across Maude's face.

"And why is that?" She didn't move as Olive started to climb. "What have I done wrong? I took in unfortunate souls like myself—others who needed an escape. I created Eidola when I was most alone, so that I wouldn't be alone anymore. I let you all in because Eidola needs life to be real. And you know what's waiting for you up there if you try to leave. You saw my audience flee, and the rest of my cast as well. Because each of them looked it in the face once long ago, and they did not wish to do it again tonight. You saw it for yourself, and you barely got away. *Death*."

Olive's foot slipped, but she regained her balance and kept climbing. The rest of the cast had seen the worm before? But that couldn't be right; they'd all insisted the cocoon held a butterfly. . . .

Maude's voice rose in anger. "Death is what brought you here, Olive Preiss. And Death is why you stayed. It's why you never wanted to leave. And you won't. Because I *will not be abandoned again*."

Her words reverberated around the trap room. Olive's hands shook, and she gripped the rungs harder.

"I'm not abandoning you. I'm saving myself."

Maude smiled wide. Wider. Impossibly wide, her lips stretching and stretching until all Olive saw below her was a gaping mouth filled with shining teeth ready to devour her whole.

36
Five Skulls

Fingers gripped her arms, and she shrieked. Felix and Juliana heaved Olive up and onto the stage. Juliana kicked the door shut, the sound echoing through the dark auditorium.

"Don't move," Felix said tersely. Juliana looked confused but did not argue, and Felix and Olive listened hard. Nothing. No sounds of Maude below. No slithering between the seats.

The rest of the cast was onstage. As Olive got to her feet, Aidan ran to her, Nadia in tow. The others stood still, their expressions ranging from confused to devastated.

"Five," Tanisha said softly, kneeling down by the remains of the cocoon. "Five skulls."

"I don't understand," said Mickey, and Val closed their eyes.

"Our first finales. When all our acts got so much better. Because . . ."

Astaire covered his face with his hands. Eli glanced at Felix, but he didn't look angry anymore. He looked defeated.

"Because we died."

At those words, a great flame burst from Mickey's torch. He held it at arm's length, startled. Then, quite suddenly, he flickered and faded, and the torch fell through his hand. Everyone watched in stunned silence as it hit the stage and rolled a few feet away.

And the laughter began.

A deep, rumbling laughter that shook the stage and dislodged one of the light fixtures. It smashed just feet from where they were huddled, spraying them with glass.

"It's Maude." Finley sounded as though he might cry. "She does all of it, all the magic."

And finally Olive understood. It hadn't been ghosts manipulating the silver rings, creating snow showers and fiery tornadoes. It had been one ghost. Maude.

She *was* Maudeville. But this theater had burned before. It could burn again. And this time, it would be destroyed completely.

Without a word, Olive lunged forward and snatched up the burning torch. The others yelled as she sprinted across the stage holding it out like a sword. She slashed at the dry, frayed curtains. In seconds they were engulfed in flames.

"Hurry!" Olive screamed, running toward the stairs as an angry roar boomed like thunder. The others followed her off the stage and past the orchestra pit. The aisles were gone; they scrambled over heaps of broken chairs, slipping over armrests and being scratched by splinters of wood.

"I'm stuck!" Juliana cried suddenly. Olive and the others hurried over to where Felix was crouched, trying to free Juliana's leg from a jumble of metal rods and ripped-up upholstery. She held the torch as close as she dared so that Felix could see better. No one spoke; there was just the sound of their labored, frightened breathing. Felix clawed at the chair wreckage. Val and Mickey attempted to help, but their hands passed through the rubble.

Val looked dumbfounded. "We could all touch every-thing before," they murmured. "Why can't we now?"

"The only reason you could before was because Maude let you," Finley replied quietly.

The hairs on the back of Olive's neck stood up as another sound reached her ears. Something far, far overhead.

Slithering.

Slowly, Olive tilted her head back. Her eyes moved from the balcony above them, to the ceiling, to the dome where Felix had clung to the chipped bronze edge. But Olive couldn't even see the edge now, just the gigantic black worm slowly uncoiling inside.

"Oh," Juliana choked, and Olive knew she saw it too. The rest of the cast gathered tightly around them, the dead forming a circle around the living.

A great crash from the stage made them all jump. The curtains had fallen, along with the catwalk. The stage was an inferno.

"*There*," Felix said triumphantly, throwing aside a

metal rod. He grabbed Juliana, and they all sprinted for the double doors, Finley flying overhead. Olive heard the slimy creature a second before it swung down from the balcony, its toothless mouth like a yawning black hole. Juliana screamed as Felix yanked her around it. He slammed into the doors and cried out in pain.

"They're locked!" Felix yelled, kicking and shoving. Olive swung the torch at the worm, which recoiled from the flames.

"This way!" She led the others around the back of the hall, heading for the side stage door. The worm slithered along the balcony overhead. And there was new movement, something that nearly caused Olive to skid to a stop.

Throughout the hall, piles of wrecked chairs were shifting. Rising. Pointy shards of wood, sharp metal rods, springs, fabric, stuffing . . . everything floated. For a few seconds, it was eerily beautiful: the hovering remains of a shattered auditorium against a backdrop of blazing curtains.

Then they began to spin, forming a funnel—a cyclone of wood and steel. And as if in slow motion, Olive watched a crooked metal bar break free of the tornado and speed toward Felix.

Olive threw the torch into the cyclone and ran straight at Felix, shoving him down. The bar smashed the back of her skull. Stars exploded in front of her eyes before everything turned to nothing.

37
They Waltzed

Nothing was lonely.

And then: a single, tiny new star burst to life. Then another. Dozens, hundreds, thousands.

They swam through space, leaving streaks of light that quickly fizzled. Constellations formed, broke apart, re-formed into new shapes: birds to fish, hammers to arrows, crowns to crosses. A ship became a man, and a lion became a little girl.

They waltzed, the girl and her father. Neither could speak, but they smiled and smiled. Words didn't exist anymore, so the girl sang a song without lyrics, and her father laughed at her silliness. They danced circles around the other constellations, faster and faster, until they were nothing but a bright, beautiful blur in the void.

38
The Delicious Wickedness

*O*live . . .

Olive?

Olive!

"She's awake!"

Her eyes opened to a world that churned like thick soup. Faces appeared, their features swirling but recognizable. Felix and Juliana. Finley too, and the rest of the cast: warm and solid and impossibly *alive*. Olive sat up, touching the back of her head. She vaguely remembered the metal bar. But the throbbing was faint, the pain as distant as the millions of stars streaking across the blackness overhead.

"What happened?" Her words came out slurred and groggy.

"We got out," Felix said. She had never seen him so happy. "Look at the theater, Olive. Really look."

Olive looked. Maudeville was a bonfire, the flames spitting and crackling in an almost comforting way. The cast cheered as the last remaining bit of the skeleton collapsed, sending yellow-orange sparks into the sky.

Beaming, Olive stood and gazed around. The city had never looked more beautiful. The sidewalks were clean, and the surrounding skyscrapers glistened in the moonlight. White lilies sprang up from every crack and crevice; the air smelled sweet and spicy and comforting.

"Olive?"

Slowly, Olive turned around. Her mother loomed over her, tall and elegant and beautiful. She opened her arms, and Olive hesitated only a moment before stepping forward.

She hugged her mother tightly around the waist, and Mrs. Preiss stroked her back. Olive apologized for the frizzies, and they both laughed. She hadn't heard her mother laugh like that in ages.

Mrs. Preiss pulled back and wiped makeup streaks from her cheeks, all black and bluish-greenish. The shade matched her dress, a very elegant dress Olive had never seen her wear before, with a full skirt and black pearl buttons. "Are those your friends?"

Olive glanced back at the cast, and her heart swelled.

"Family," she told her mother. "Can they be our family now?"

It was an absurd question to ask. Mrs. Preiss wouldn't let Olive drop a nickel into a busker's hat, much less invite a group of vagabonds into the penthouse. But to Olive's amazement, she smiled.

"Of course, sweetheart. Of course." Her voice dripped with syrupy sweetness.

Fresh tears of relief and gratitude sprang to Olive's eyes. Her mother's smile grew wider. Her eyes glinted with hunger. Olive took a step back.

Imagine the delicious wickedness Laurel Preiss would unleash as a villain.

"Mom?" she whispered.

"Yes, darling?"

Olive began to shake. But her mother kept smiling.

W i d e r   a n d   w
                                                i
                                                  d
                                                    e
                                                      r.

39
Real

"Olive . . ."

"Olive?"

"Olive!"

The stars were back. But these stars weren't waltzing in the night sky. They were rattling around in Olive's skull, a hailstorm of bright, jagged stars piercing her brain, blinding her. The ringing in her ears was somehow ascending and descending in pitch at the same time. She tried to inhale, but her lungs were stuffed with damp dustrags.

Panicked, Olive sat upright and gasped for air. There was a cry of relief, and she caught a glimpse of Juliana's tear-streaked face before her friend tackled her in a hug.

"Let her breathe, Jules," said Felix, but he sounded intensely relieved. Olive blinked rapidly, wiping her eyes as Juliana pulled away. The back of Olive's skull throbbed terribly. She tried to ignore it. This was real. It was agonizing and nauseating, but it was *real*.

"Where are we?" Her voice sounded thick and warbled in her head.

"Rehearsal room." Val appeared at her side. Olive craned her neck to look around and was rewarded with a fresh wave of nausea. But through the haze of pain, she counted the others. Finley floated quietly next to his brother and sister, while Knuckles and his hands—still and solemn—hovered near the door with the seamstresses. Astaire huddled next to them, real tears smearing the painted one in a black streak down his cheek. Mickey, Val, Eli, and Tanisha stood close together too.

Olive could see straight through them all. She wasn't sure if it was because now she knew they were ghosts, or because *they* knew. But either way, her heart ached at the sight.

Aidan stood apart from them. He clung to Nadia and carefully avoided looking at his fellow cast members, his expression a mix of confusion and fear. And he was solid.

Because he was alive, Olive realized. Like her, Aidan had never had his first finale. He'd never been taken by the worm.

Aidan was *alive,* and so were Olive and Felix and Juliana. But not for long, not unless they escaped.

"The theater's on fire," Olive said thickly. She could still taste the smoke in her mouth. "We have to get out."

"Are you sure that's what you want, darling?"

Olive shot to her feet, ignoring fresh stabs of pain in her head. Aidan whimpered and buried his face in Nadia's hair.

Dozens of Maudes smiled at them from the mirrors. But there was no Maude in the room. Just reflections. Her deep voice came from all around them.

"The theater has burned before," the Maudes told Olive. "And yet I'm still here. If you don't want to be my star, I'll find another. This city is filled with desperate people who need to escape."

Val turned away from the mirrors, eyes blazing. "Enough," they said. "Let's go. Olive's right—we can leave if we want to. Living or dead."

The Maudes laughed. "Be my guest." Then the reflections vanished.

Shaking, Olive took a few steps back. There was a sharp *snap,* then another, and another. The mirrors were fracturing, great cracks rippling out from the center like a jagged spiderweb.

No one wasted any time. They sprinted to the doors a split second before the mirrors exploded. Shards of glass sliced the backs of Olive's arms and legs as she fled the rehearsal room with the others, heading back to the hall.

40

A Lowered Curtain

The ghosts led the way, streaming past the dorm. There was a series of thuds, and a headboard flew out, passing through Mickey and aiming straight for Olive. She ducked, and it smashed into the wall. Bedposts and blankets followed, swinging at heads, attempting to strangle necks. The kitchen launched an attack of forks and knives and rotten food that splattered and clattered all over the hall, and Olive barely had time to wonder about the deafening *crunch* that followed when the oven smashed through the wall, mangled pipes dragging behind it. The entire thing hovered briefly over their heads before the oven door fell open, raining down dead, partially roasted rats and maggots.

Bile rose in Olive's throat, and she choked back a scream. Grabbing Aidan—who was paralyzed with fear—by the shirt, she dragged him into the stairwell. The others followed, no one uttering a word as they headed to the side entrance Olive had propped open for Felix just hours earlier. Finding it closed, they pushed and pushed, but it wouldn't budge.

"The lobby," Olive said hoarsely, already heading back down the hall. Behind her, Juliana groaned.

"What's the point?" she wailed. "You know she won't let us out those doors either." But she followed, clinging to Felix's hand.

Wisps of smoke curled up from under the double doors. The crackling roar of the fire raging in the auditorium was muffled, but the lobby itself was eerily calm. It looked as it had the night Olive had run away, only worse: thick cobwebs all but obscuring the chandeliers, black spiders skittering across the ceiling and down the cracked columns. Everything was coated in dust and ash, even the portraits. The painted Maudes wore ravenous grins.

Aidan, Felix, Juliana, and Olive huddled together, staring at the doors. The lobby suddenly seemed very, very long.

"Oh," Finley said suddenly, and they turned, startled. Olive's breath caught in her throat. Finley was fainter, much fainter. All the ghosts were, including the cast. Two examined her hands, which were barely visible. She smiled. It was the first time Olive had seen her look calm.

"What's going on?" Juliana whispered.

Slam.

Everyone spun around and stared at the auditorium doors.

Slam. Slam.

Crash!

Flames shot out into the lobby, surrounding what looked like a black hole. It was as if the auditorium was now the very pit of hell. Then the hole lunged forward, and Olive felt the worm's hot breath.

"Run!" she cried. They sprinted across the lobby, the great worm thrashing blindly behind them. One by one, the marble columns splintered and began to fall with an earsplitting, teeth-rattling crash. The Maude portraits were no longer smiling, their faces twisted in silent screams as the cobweb-covered chandeliers ripped out of the ceiling and launched themselves at the children. Olive and the others had nearly reached the doors when the final column began to fall. Olive's heart plummeted—they couldn't all clear it. Someone would surely be crushed—

But Finley soared high overhead, straight at the column. He didn't pass through it. He *caught* it, held it effortlessly, his expression of surprise mirroring those below him. He smiled, looking rather delighted at his own cleverness and skill.

And then he threw the column at the doors.

They splintered open as if made of matchsticks. Olive scrambled over the column and practically threw Aidan and Nadia outside before helping the others through. They hurried down the steps and stopped on the street.

The theater was crumbling in on itself, black smoke drifting up into the night sky. The ghosts hovered over the last step.

"How did you do that with the column?" Juliana asked, her voice cracking as she gazed at Finley. He beamed.

"Maude isn't the only person buried at the theater," he said. "I'm down there too. Everyone else died in Eidola during their first finale, but I didn't. Because I saw *you*, Felix. I'm a part of the theater, just like Maude."

"Did you all know?" Olive looked pleadingly from one cast member to another. "Did you know what would happen to me and Aidan during the finale?"

"No!" Tanisha cried immediately. "No, Olive, I swear. . . . It was a butterfly. None of us saw the worm during our first finales. We saw . . ."

"We saw what we wanted to see," Eli finished. "Just like we saw Eidola." He turned to Felix, lips quivering. "That's why we tried so hard to keep you out. You didn't just remind Finley of what was real. You reminded all of us."

"We're all so sorry," Val added softly. Mickey nodded in agreement, his eyes red-rimmed.

Felix took a deep breath. "It's okay. I understand. But now . . ." His desperate gaze fell on his brother's ghost. "You aren't trapped here, are you?"

Finley shook his head. "I was never trapped. I stayed here after I died because I wanted to be with you and Juliana."

"None of us is trapped." Knuckles floated forward, his hands hovering at his wrists. "Quite the opposite. The theater is almost gone. We have to leave too."

Tanisha let out a choked sob, and Val placed a hand on her shoulder.

"It's okay. We can let go," they said, looking around at the others. "We can *all* let go."

Finley smiled at his brother and sister. "It's okay," he whispered. "I'll be okay." Juliana let out a whimper, and Felix grabbed her hand. A distant roar sounded from the theater as the flames shot higher, smoke billowing out in all directions.

The group gathered one last time: the Morellas, the cast, Knuckles, the seamstresses. Olive wiped her eyes, listening to the sniffles and sobs and whispered words of comfort as everyone said their goodbyes. But she couldn't. She didn't want to—it would be too final. Olive preferred to hope she would see them again. After all, a lowered curtain was not content to remain that way forever. It was just waiting to rise again.

Then it happened: the theater collapsed with a final roar, and the resulting gust of hot wind scattered the ghosts like dust in the air.

Tears streamed freely down Olive's face. She wanted to

say something, offer some comfort to Felix and Juliana. But no words were adequate, and so she stood there in silence as they hugged and cried.

They had each other, Olive told herself. They'd suffered a terrible loss, but they were still a family, the two of them. She placed a hand on Aidan's shoulder as he wept into Nadia's hair.

Four children and one puppet huddled close together, watching in silence as the remains of Maudeville burned. There was no sign of the worm. No sign of Maude. Just an old theater that had been their home when they had no other place to go.

"The carnival," Felix told Olive and Aidan, his voice tired and hoarse. He wrapped his arm protectively around his sister's shoulders. "That's where we're going. You could come with us, both of you. I'm sure they'd be interested in a ventriloquist and a singer."

In the distance, sirens wailed, growing louder and louder. Olive clenched and unclenched her hands in her lap. She could stay with Felix and Juliana, Aidan and Nadia. She could be a part of this family. It was sorely tempting.

But Olive wasn't sure it was what she really wanted. Overhead, endless constellations twinkled through the smoke. She stared up at them and found a messy heart.

A fire truck screeched to a halt down the street, followed by several police cars. Olive wiped her face and squinted. There was another car too. A familiar car.

"You called," she remembered suddenly. "You called the number on that flyer."

Felix nodded. "I told her you were here."

Olive drew a deep, shaky breath. "I'll be right back," she promised.

She stood, smoothing her hair and brushing off her nightgown. Memories of a life that seemed longer ago than it should resurfaced, sharp and real: harsh criticism and disapproving looks; stargazing and secret paychecks; pink callused fingers, one with the imprint of a ring still pressed into the skin. The hole in Olive's chest was raw and open once more, but she was glad. She had tried to stitch it up too soon, and all by herself. She would not make that mistake again. A car door slammed. A familiar, frantic voice called her name, and Olive ran toward her mother as fast as she could.

In the heart of a monstrous city, firefighters hurried toward the blazing ruins of a theater. A crowd began to gather, some to gawk, others offering help and comfort to the survivors. And for the first time in more than a year, a girl and her mother embraced, laughing and crying beneath a night sky filled with infinite stars.

Acknowledgments

Forever indebted to Diane Landolf and Sarah Davies for finding this story's heart, which I thought I had so carefully hidden under the floorboards.

```
                            1
                1          1
                1      1
              1    1             'tis a gala night
                 1            within the lonesome latter years!
          an angel throng,    lo!  bewinged, bedight in veils, and drowned
       in tears, sit in a theatre, to see   a play of hopes and fears, while the orchestra
      breathes fitfully the music of the   spheres, mimes, in the form of god on high, mutter
   and mumble low, and hither and thither   fly—mere puppets they, who come and go at bidding
   of vast formless things that shift the scenery   to and fro, flapping from out their condor wings
 invisible wo! that motley drama—oh, be sure it   shall not be forgot! with its phantom chased
    for evermore by a crowd that seize it not,   through a circle that ever returneth in to
       the self-same spot, and much   of madness, and more of sin
             and horror    the soul of the plot.
         but see, amid the    mimic rout, a crawling
       shape intrude! a blood - red thing that writhes
     from out the scenic solitude!—it writhes!—it writhes!—with mortal
     pangs the mimes become its food, and seraphs sob at vermin
     fangs in human gore inbued. out—out are the lights—out all!
     and, over each quivering form, the curtain, a funeral pall,
            comes down with    the rush of a storm,
            while the angels,    all pallid and wan,
              uprising,        unveiling,
               affirm          that the
                play            is the
                tra             gedy,
                man,            and
                its             hero
                the             w
                con             o
                qu              r
                er              m
                o
                r
```

—Edgar Allan Poe, "The Conqueror Worm"